RUN LIKE THE WIND

THE SHTF SERIES BOOK THREE

L.L. AKERS

SCORCHED EARTH PUBLISHING, LLC

Ten thousand people, maybe more...
People talking without speaking,
People hearing without listening,
People writing songs, that voices never share
and no one dared...
Disturb the sound of silence..."

~ Simon & Garfunkel

RUN LIKE THE WIND

Book **Three** of the chart-topping ***SHTF Series*** is here, and early readers say it's the best one yet!

It's still TEOTWAWKI for Tucker.

The power grid went down a month ago, and mayhem continues when food is depleted or raided, and water sources are running dry. As resources grow scarce, regular people begin to slide into savagery, especially when Tucker and Katie lose one of their own at Tullymore. Without rule of law, justice is the new law of the land, and they fall back to *an eye for an eye.*

Can Grayson and Olivia hold it together as their group grows larger, but one of them takes a bullet?

At Grayson's farm, training is in full force, but not everyone is comfortable with the wild, wild west their world has become. When one of their own takes a bullet, and Olivia is to blame, they must all come together before they fall apart.

Is this really the end of their world as they know it?

The streets are either eerily barren, or filled with hunger-crazed mobs. Homes are left with nothing more than blackened stone and burnt-out dreams when the help *they thought* had arrived does more damage, than good. But F'kn Puck is on a mission to finally be a hero; he'll either survive and persevere, or die trying.

Death is imminent, and bullets and blood fill their days as they *Run Like the Wind* in book three of *The SHTF Series*, a post-apocalyptic thriller packed with Action & Adventure.

The SHTF Series:
Book 1: Fight Like a Man
Book 2: Shoot Like a Girl
Book 3: Run Like the Wind

Sign up to the Shit (hit the fan) List here: http://eepurl.com/bMDLT1 to be notified via email when the next SHTF book comes out.

To my son, Zach.

PROLOGUE

FK'N PUCK SQUEEZED his eyes tight when the gun bellowed, announcing its displeasure at not being respected. GrayMan had given him the lecture: *Respect the gun. Always respect the gun. No goofing around.*

He'd known it was coming.

He saw it.

At first, Mama Dee had told him it was Déjà vu; nothing special, all people had it at some time or the other. But since Puck had bumped his head—or since his head had been bumped—he had it a lot, and he knew it was more than just that.

Then she'd called them seizures. She took him to a doctor who put him on a table that rolled him into a box. It shook and scared him; made him feel trapped.

The doctor gave him medicine.

The medicine was piled up in his room now at Mama Dee's house, in a tiny hole in his mattress.

It made his head feel funny.

Funnier than the seizures did.

He'd rather see things coming *sometimes*, than be confused *all* the time.

He just wished he was smart enough to *stop* the seeing.

Mama Dee said to *never* talk about it. That's why he drew the pictures. He couldn't block out this *knowing*; couldn't make it stop bothering him...poking at his brain and keeping him awake at night, unless he talked about it, or put it on paper. But he hadn't had time for this one. When the knowing came, he'd only wanted to stop it, before it had *become*.

For a moment—after the *boom*—there was dead silence.

And then, the air erupted in a cacophony of screams, scattering the otherwise quiet of the farm. The cicadas stopped chirping, the chickens stopped chattering. The birds perched on high limbs, peering down over their fat bosoms with darting, cautious eyes at the river of blood, before frantically flying away in fright.

At the women.

Olivia, Gabby, Tina, Tarra—even Graysie.

They were *all* there.

He'd known they would be. That was why he'd insisted on tagging along with the women today, instead of with GrayMan and Jake, or Elmer. He'd felt GrayMan's disappointment that he'd not chosen to do *A Man Thing*. But Mama Dee said never to talk about it, so he couldn't tell GrayMan *why* he'd wanted to be with the girls.

Puck's hands slid down and he slowly opened his wet eyes—ever so slowly—already knowing what he'd see. Dreading it. But it was worse than he'd already *seen*.

So much blood.

He could hear his father's angry voice groaning, '*Fuckin' Puck*,' and see the disappointed shake of his head. He could feel it in his bones—and his aching heart. He'd failed at something, yet again.

His real dad was gone.

But GrayMan was gonna be mad at him now, too.

1

THE FARM

FEAR KNOTTED his stomach as Grayson sat alone with his head in his hands in a collapsible lawn chair in the barn, not realizing daybreak had come until Jenny nudged him, and not too gently. She had a ferocious internal *hangry* clock and if he didn't feed her soon, she'd take a flirty nip out of him.

Or she'd head to Puck's window to beg, and wake up the whole house.

He wasn't used to sharing his quiet place with anyone, but especially a grumpy, mule-headed donkey. He nudged her right back. "Just a few more minutes, Jenny. Leave me alone, girl."

Ozzie, who had been asleep at his feet, stood and pushed himself between his master and the impatient donkey. Even the dog knew he needed this time alone, to get his head straight before rousting the others.

Grayson was afraid—scared of *failing* his family and friends—but was trying to keep his salty humor, and not let anyone see the anxiety that was keeping him from slumber.

Ozzie felt it, though. The dog gave a low whine and nudged him, too, as though to say *snap out of it, Hooman.*

With little to no privacy now, this was where he came to try to gather his thoughts and bury his worries and fears deep inside, from anyone who might be looking. He was responsible for everyone here, and bellyaching about it wouldn't change a thing, even if nearly everyone else was acting as though it was all going to be okay.

He didn't begrudge them their hopefulness. All the way out in the country like they were, it was easy for most of them to forget the world around them was fubar.

But not for him. For him, reality was staring him in the face every moment, around the clock, as their food ran low and their fuel ran lower.

He rubbed Ozzie's head. "It's okay, boy. Lay down."

Ozzie curled up once again at his feet, leaving him to battle the barrage of *what ifs* and *if they could's* once more. There was no peace from the nagging worry that things were about to get much worse. The facts were the facts...and every day was one day closer to their little haven possibly being set upon by a despairing Golden Horde.

One month had gone by and still no power. The city was in chaos. No information was coming from the government. No military had been spotted. Food was scarce to nonexistent for most people, water was hard to come by for many—luckily, he was prepared with a well and a hand pump—but few people had been prepared for a disaster of this level.

The violent scramble to empty the shelves in the grocery stores lasted no more than a few days, ending in bloodshed frequently, and inciting looting, violence and rioting. There were no refills for critical medicines, and no more incoming fuel for vehicles to venture out further to find any of the basic needs of the average American.

People were extremely hungry, sick, and tired.

They were desperate and mad.

The city was being stripped of every critical resource, and recklessly razed to the ground. Soon, those desperate people would be headed out on foot toward the country, moving on to greener pastures.

Literally.

And they would be *dangerous*.

Big Pharma had added to the mayhem by helping to breed an entire generation of impulsive pill-heads and junkies, all willing to kill or die for their next fix, and unable to get it; they were almost more dangerous than the roving gangs. Most of the elderly soon perished without their life-sustaining medications, and while he wasn't sure if the power outage was everywhere, he had to assume it was, since no help had come yet. So, what was left of America was probably an anxious, and nearly hopeless nation, the remnants of families who never thought their great country could be torn asunder in such a short time, just by flipping the light switch.

No one had believed it could get *this* bad, this fast.

Grayson sighed heavily and stood up. He stretched. What he wouldn't give for a straight eight of sleep.

True to her nature, and not liking to be forgotten, Jenny swung her head in and took a small nip at his backside, her reminder that she was waiting.

"Whoa," Grayson yelled, rubbing his hind quarters and turning quickly, holding one hand up to ward her off, only to find her big lips pulled back from her square, yellow teeth in a silly, innocent smile.

She brayed her apologies at him, pleading with a fluttering of her lashes.

He answered her with thin lips and a shake of his head,

but did her bidding. After feeding Jenny, he hurried from the barn, tamping down his anxiety and setting his jaw with pure grit. He squinted at the big orange orb—seeming higher than it should be. Maybe he had caught a few winks after all. Olivia would be nagging at him for sleeping in the barn if she knew.

He grimaced, knowing that big ball of heat would attack him in no more than fifty feet, the thick and muggy air leaving his shirt damp in the sweltering Carolina summer heat.

Grayson glanced back at the barn, noticing the sun had already been plying its trade against it too, lying in wait for him... it was laying claim to the old red paint, bright and early. He could almost hear the siding peel and curl as he headed to the house through the long clover.

The smell of chicken shit and hay tickled his nose as he passed through, glad that when the chicken feed ran out, they could graze here, and if they couldn't eat fast enough, it wouldn't go to waste—Jenny would eat it once it died and dried.

Amazing what a month without mowing would do. He could barely see the chickens as they hurried to cut paths through the tall weeds, pecking at the dirt to look for that early worm, fly, or bug that lurked in the grass.

All around the farm it was still quiet, other than the cicada's chirping their song, the birds tweeting, and the chickens clucking. His dark mood was slowly dissipating. The quiet sounds of the countryside were already working on his spirits. A balm to his soul.

A real farm was probably livelier, but his was only a homestead with a farmhouse, the barn, and a small-ish garden. It was more of a hobby-farm.

They just liked to *call it* the farm.

Although he knew they were blessed—especially now—to have this place, he wished it were a real farm, with a sounder of pigs and a herd of cows; fresh milk and meat fattening up on the bone; a rooster to make more little chicks who'd make more eggs and meat, and rows and rows of corn and other abundant foods to be harvested.

If only I'd been more prepared...

Lately though, his place had come alive with life. Where before it was just he and his wife, Olivia, and their dog, Ozzie, and a home-visit every other weekend from Graysie—she'd been away at college when the grid went down—now they had her back, *and* the addition of another teenager named Puck; this one male, the stubborn female donkey, a cantankerous old man named Elmer, a piglet wearing a ridiculous tutu, Olivia's twin sister, Gabby, and her husband, Jake, and two more spitfires of the female persuasion: Tina and Tarra.

Nine humans, a donkey, a dog and a pig—and some chickens.

He stole another glance at the sun and realized he really had been lost in his thoughts much longer than he'd thought. Morning was slipping away and things weren't usually this quiet at this time of day.

The glare of the ratty old pop-up camper shining back at him with the door hanging wide open, framed by torn and tattered curtains hanging limp said the workday hadn't yet started. He'd expect Tina and Tarra to be up and nearly finished cleaning up the nasty, cramped thing that he and Jake had found in Puck and Mama Dee's yard by now. They'd pulled it over with the tractor, surprised that the wheels hadn't rotted off yet, and had made some minor repairs.

It wasn't the Taj Mahal, but it'd do to sleep in, after

Olivia put in some clean bedding and added her finishing touches to it.

They were running out of room in the house and he was tired of tripping over people. It hadn't taken much to entice Tina and Tarra to agree to sleep in the camper, which would also alleviate some tension between them and his wife. Having five women in the house was no walk in the park. Two less would help.

He rounded the corner and found his family on the front porch. Nearly the whole group, minus himself, Elmer and Jake, sat around looking like death eatin' on a chicken bone. The day was already stacking up to be a scorcher. Tina and Tarra sat on the porch swing, it barely moving in the soupy air. Olivia sat on the steps, Gabby in a rocking chair, and Graysie and Puck were leaned up against the wall, legs splayed out in front of them.

Grayson dug deep to shake off his mood, and find his humor. "Y'all are like a bunch of dog pecker gnats, hovering around on a hot sticky day. Where's your get-up-and-go? There's plenty of work to be done."

Several sets of eyes narrowed and cut toward Olivia, who sat hunched over, her chin in her hands and elbows on knees. Grayson studied the group: sleepy, grumpy, afflicted with pain? They all had their eyes scrunched up as though they were nursing headaches.

Oh.

He cringed.

The coffee finally ran out.

That alone was an apocalyptic event.

2

THE FARM

Before he could put his thoughts to words, Tina snapped a snarky response, "My get-up-and-go has *got up and left* with the coffee that your *wife* gave away."

Tarra elbowed her in warning. "What Tina *means* is we're all suffering from withdrawals. Our heads ache, and we just don't feel like working yet."

She too probably wanted to point the finger at Olivia, but they were guests here, and this *was* Olivia and Grayson's house. Lately, she had kept it better in check than Tarra had. While Olivia hadn't made them feel particularly welcome, Grayson and Jake had insisted they stay, at least until they could devise a plan to get them home safely. Tina and Tarra had been in from out of town for a shooting competition when the grid went down, and by pure happenstance had come across Jake.

Actually, Jake had come across them, camped out in the woods.

They'd recognized the logo on the hat he'd worn as TSS: The Shooting Sisterhood; a Facebook group that they belonged to, where they were online friends with Jake's wife, Gabby.

Olivia sighed. "I'm sorry," she said, again. She'd already apologized numerous times for donating some of the prepped food buckets and bins from Grayson's larder to the church—including the coffee. What they'd been able to scrounge up since then had lasted until now, but they were fresh out. "I can't believe in all that stuff we found in Elmer's truck, there wasn't any coffee."

After the attack on the farm by Trunk and his gang, Jake had sent Smalls walking. He was the lone survivor, and was in bad shape with a gunshot wound. No one had seen a vehicle, but Grayson had felt sure there was one, somewhere, and Smalls would leave the same way he got here.

Jake was too soft. They should'a sent the man to nap.

A dirt nap.

But Grayson had been wrong. Smalls *had* left on foot. The one silver lining to the gang showing up here had revealed itself few days later, when out on a walk, Elmer did come across the vehicle that Grayson had felt sure was there —Elmer's own truck—parked in the woods, filled with his own belongings: some food, mostly in mason jars prepared and hand-packed by his dearly departed wife, and a few other odds and ends that the group was happy to see added to their larder and supplies.

But most of all, Elmer's prized pair of Baby Desert Eagles; The Beagles, he called them. Grayson had made sure through the years that the family had acquired weapons of the same caliber so they could combine ammunition if they ever needed to. It was a lucky coincidence that Beagles were the same, too.

The food they'd found hadn't made up for what was given away, but on top of what was left, it was enough to add to the larder and feed this ever-growing group for an additional few weeks.

But no coffee.

While he understood everyone's frustration, and their fear, he could cut his wife some slack. Olivia had passed many years now as the wife of a prepper, and they'd never had any real occasion to use the preps that Grayson obsessed about, and periodically added to, or rotated out.

Like most people, she never really believed a true disaster would ever hit *them*. Never thought she'd see a day when you couldn't run to the store to pick up the essentials, and she sure didn't know one of the totes she'd given away held their entire supply of extra coffee.

She'd have never given *that* away.

Coffee—or lack of it—was her kryptonite.

She was a sheeple. Pure and simple.

Of course she hadn't thought that the *one time* she borrowed from the prepping larder—to save her some time in doing her own shopping for the charity church food drive—that they'd actually *really* need it.

But damn, he loved this woman. She was also a bit spoiled; and he'd not deny that he helped make her that way.

His life was incomplete after the loss of his first wife—Graysie's mother—due to a shit hit the fan disaster, which was one of the reasons he did prep and prepare now. It had truly been TEOTWAWKI for him and Graysie, but Olivia later filled that void in his life, healing the hole left in his heart, and putting the pieces of his soul back together.

As far as he was concerned, once he got past the initial anger, she could give away every last damn crumb of food and every tiny pinch of coffee they had. As long as she and his daughter, Graysie, were still okay, he'd deal with it, somehow. At least they were together. And so far, they were safe and fed.

It's not the end of the world—again.

At least, not yet.

He stepped up beside her, turned, and sat down, showing some unity—if not forgiveness—again. He knew her heart was in the right place. Olivia would give the shirt off her back to help someone. She was a *giver*. Couldn't be helped. That was something he'd always loved about her. It was just bad timing, this time.

Jake turned up, looking weirdly jumpy, and carrying a well-used leather satchel of tools. He avoided eye contact with Grayson as he found a seat on the porch.

Grayson lifted his shirt up to wipe at the dirty sweat on his face. "So, the java finally ran out, huh?"

Olivia nodded sadly. "I told everybody last week I was near to scraping the bottom of the can. I guess we weren't expecting it to be this bad though." She rubbed her head.

His own head was pounding, too, but not any worse than his bad tooth. He'd love to lounge around and nurse all that ailed him; sitting still helped relieve the pressure some. But there was no time to sit still. There was firewood to cut and split, more work to do on the camper, food to be cooked, laundry to be washed and hung, and the *big job* coming up.

They'd need all hands on-deck for that.

How am I gonna motivate these people to get started without coffee?

The air grew thick with a quiet tension. Grayson turned to look at Puck, giving him a half-smile and getting a little wave and big cheesy grin in return. At least Puck wasn't affected. The kid didn't drink coffee. He was fine; full of energy as usual, recovered from his bee stings now, and almost fully recovered from his gunshot wound, too.

Built like an ox, healthy as a horse, the kid was a fast healer.

Puck had taken to hanging out wherever Graysie or Olivia was—had become somewhat attached to both and seemed a part of the family now. But had he raised him, he wouldn't be following the women around. *Nope.* He was going to have to work harder on teaching the boy to work like a man now that he was under his care.

"Puck, have you seen Elmer today?" he asked, already knowing the answer. Puck kept his eye on the old man, too; almost to the point of stalking.

"Yeah, GrayMan. He's sitting in his chair by the tree-line," Puck answered.

Since Elmer's arrival, after the loss of his wife, Edith, he'd taken to sitting in a lawn chair at the edge of the yard, facing away from the house, and looking into the woods. Every morning, the first thing Elmer did when he sat down was light a cigarette. He smoked that one cancer-stick in silent thought, and then spent the day quiet and alone. Everybody dealt with grief in their own way and this was his way, so they tried to give him his space.

Several times Grayson had wondered if that was the right thing to do though. Surely the man was getting lonely to talk to *someone*. He'd mosey over, intending to try to draw him out and chew the fat, only to find him already in a conversation.

With Edith.

So, he left him alone, to deal with his demons the best way he could. Puck however, spied on him at all times. The kid was very empathetic and was drawn to the old man. Grayson could see on Puck's face the desire to pull up a chair and talk his ears off, but somehow the kid held back, satisfied with knowing where Elmer was, and keeping an eye on him from afar.

Elmer usually followed the smell of supper back to the house just as the plates were handed out. He ate in silence, thanked them for the food, and then walked back to his chair outside. He returned late at night to sleep on the couch, refusing to take one of the three beds.

"He talking to Edith out there again today?" Grayson asked Puck.

"No, sir. Not today. He smoked his cigarette, and then built a campfire, and then washed some plants," Puck answered in the funny way he talked. "And then cooked some coffee-bean-stuff in a box, and then boiled it over the fire in water, and then poured it into a cup and drank it and then smacked his lips and then sighed really loud," Puck answered innocently, followed by a wide, proud smile at giving such a full report to *GrayMan*.

And then? Grayson was dying to ask, but kept it to himself, hiding it behind a smirk.

All eyes widened and faces perked up. The ladies stood in unison. "Coffee?" Olivia asked. "Are you sure?"

Puck shrugged. "It smelled like coffee. And then it was brown after he cooked it. He drank it out of a coffee mug, and then it made him smile a little bit."

Okay, the '*and then*' was getting on his nerves a bit now...

That was enough evidence for the ladies. As one, they all hurried off the porch, shoving past Grayson. He flinched at the stampede, tucking his shoulders in tight, and laughed. Headed toward Elmer's quiet place was Olivia in the lead, followed by Gabby and then Tina and Tarra, with Graysie behind them, waving a hand back at Puck to follow her.

Grayson knew *for a fact* that Elmer didn't have any coffee beans. He came with *nothing*, in his hurry to warn the girls that Trunk and his boys were on the way. And there hadn't been any in his truck that the gang had arrived in. He'd searched through everything himself. He hoped whatever it was that Elmer was cooking up, was a' plenty and would pass muster with the girls.

3

THE FARM

ELMER EASED up from his chair, his old knees creaking loudly, and stood. The wrinkles in his face were creased with grief and dirt. More dirt than grief, as he'd made his peace with Edith and his failure to protect her from the motorcycle gang led by Trunk. The pain of her loss was nothing compared to the pain of knowing what they'd put her through before she passed.

Branded.

The Wild Ones used their initials: TWO, to proudly ink themselves like a bunch of randy peacocks. It was *just* ink—a regular tattoo. But on their women, or anyone that crossed them, they used the number '2,' burned into the skin with a sizzling hot steel branding iron to mark them.

Like an animal.

Her demise, thrown alive, into a grave with a dead body, after being marked like a wayward cow, was almost more than he could bear to think about. The thought of her terror brought tears to his cloudy eyes and a pain to his old heart.

But a few days ago, he'd awoken with a sense of forgiveness. Edith never was one to hold a grudge. He'd had many conversations with her lately, some overheard by Grayson and Puck. He felt sure they thought he'd lost his mind, but Edith wasn't talking back to him.

She was dead for Pete's sake. How could she?

He was doing all the talking.

Working it out in his mind.

Watching this motley crew, as they watched him, he'd seen them suffer though the withdrawals of caffeine, putting the blame on Grayson's wife for giving away the coveted coffee supply. He'd shrugged off the lethargy and headaches himself; what pain could be worse than the loss of your wife?

He was over it, but that didn't mean he couldn't be comforted by a hot cup of joe—or something that looked and smelled, maybe even tasted, like it.

He'd snuck off and foraged for Chicory plants. He'd found plenty alongside the road—and was also tickled to find his own truck full of food and supplies, hand-delivered by the monsters that'd killed his wife—but the Chicory he'd found by the road wasn't safe. It had probably ingested exhaust and fumes from cars, and more than likely would do more harm than good.

He'd had to walk further and further each day on his hunt to find some not exposed to the modern poisons all around them. He found more far enough off the road to be safe, and once he'd dug up a good many, he'd harvested the roots, washed them off, scraped them, chopped them up into small pieces, and then soaked them in water while he built a solar oven to roast them in.

For the oven, he'd swiped one of Olivia's wooden planters off her back porch; he was surprised she hadn't noticed yet, but looking at the dead plant inside, it was obvious she'd forgotten all about it. The planter wasn't very big at 24 inches square, but big enough. He'd tossed out the dried-up dead plant, rinsed it out, then insulated the inside of the wooden box with a stack of crumpled and crushed newspapers, using silicone glue to adhere it to the wood as a liner on the interior of the box.

Then he'd made a smaller box out of scrap wood he'd dug up from the barn, and covered the inside and the outside of the smaller box with aluminum, and nested it inside the wooden planter, making sure there was no space between the outside of the smaller box and the newspaper liner.

That was the body of the oven.

For the window/door on the top where the sun would shine through, he'd swiped the glass and frame from the one and only window in Grayson's barn. It came out of a small tack room, that looked as though it hadn't been used in years as more than a closet; it was covered in dust and cobwebs. So, he felt justified in re-purposing it.

He plugged the hole he'd left with plywood.

He had *some* manners.

With a few screws and hinges he'd rummaged out of Grayson's shop, he'd made the window into a door of sorts, and attached that to the top of the planter.

Then he cut four even pieces of plywood for the 'sun funnel,' covering them with tin foil—nearly slicing his finger off with the sharp edges—and attached them to all four sides of the planter at an angle, so that the sun would reflect from every which way, back down onto the glass door.

The light went through the oven's door and heated up the air in the interior with the reflective tin foil. At the same time, the insulation layer of newspaper kept the same heat inside of the oven.

He'd attached a thermometer—swiped from Olivia's junk drawer—to the oven when it was finished and tested it out, putting a layer of the Chicory roots at the bottom of an open-topped Dutch oven and placing it inside. Surprisingly, during the hottest part of the day, the temperature hit 350 degrees. He'd roasted the Chicory roots for many hours, until they were dark brown and dry, and then let them cool. He then boiled them over his camp fire in an old dented metal pot also from Olivia's kitchen, steeped them in the water for a few moments, and finally, strained the concoction with a bandana.

He held his coffee up in the air and took a sniff. "A fine cup of coffee," he muttered aloud. *Or close enough.*

Looking over his shoulder at the small crowd of crazy-eyed females marching across the yard, he pulled the old towel off the stump, revealing five half-pint Mason jars of dried, roasted Chicory Root.

No one could say he didn't earn his keep. He might not have brought anything with him—but fate had brought his supplies anyway, meager that they were. And his old eyes might not be the best behind a scope, his legs and arms had seen their better days, and his short-term memory wasn't sharp, but he wasn't totally useless.

This, he could do.

So far, he had one small jar for each of the women. He assumed they'd share with the gentleman folk, and maybe take charge of having it ready and steaming in the mornings.

It wouldn't give them their caffeine, though, which in his mind was a good thing. But it'd give them a mental-kick in their rumps that they sorely needed to start their day.

He threw back the last dregs in the cup, even swallowing the loose grounds—dirt? —from the bottom. He grimaced, just as Olivia and the other ladies arrived, and picked at his teeth with a dirty yellowed fingernail.

Those roots could 'a been cleaner.

The women stared at the jars in amazement, willing their eyes to believe it was coffee. Grayson arrived with Jake at his heels, and they both stepped up to examine the solar oven.

"Now, before you get too excited, it's not coffee. But it's *like* coffee. Close as we're gonna get. Give this batch a try. For the next batch, I'll need a scrub brush. And a grinder. Maybe even a real strainer," Elmer grumbled. "Grinding the roots before boiling them would make it even more like real coffee. Maybe you can do better with it. You're quite the home-maker," he said, as he handed Olivia her jar, and a compliment, at the same time.

She cradled both to her chest.

The woman was a bit fragile, but she was quite the cook. Not in Edith's league, but close.

Elmer belched and swiped at his mouth. "Not as good as real cup of joe, but good enough." He drank his joe straight —black—but he'd also tested a cup with a bit of nutmeg and cinnamon, assuming the ladies probably liked that fluffy foo-foo Starbucks stuff, and would need to doctor it up. That was good, too. *For the women, anyway.*

But he'd take away the man card from any of the boys who attempted to lighten up his joe. Same as he'd do if they were his own boys.

Which by this time, they were.

He wasn't volunteering the fact that the concoction didn't have caffeine in it. If they wanted to *assum*e it did, he'd let them believe what they *needed* to believe.

They'd nearly beat the caffeine addiction, anyway. And while he *could* show them how to make Holly Berry Tea and get caffeinated again, it was dangerous. If not done exactly right, it could cause diarrhea and vomiting, and he hadn't seen this family's paper collection yet, but in a grid-down situation, he'd think it best to avoid multiple trips and long rests on the john.

Plus, the tea was made from the *leaves* of the *American Holly Tree*, not the fruit; and he didn't trust that kid, Fuckin' Puck, not to pop one of the delicious-looking red berries into his pie hole. Seemed like a good kid, but maybe just a sandwich short of a picnic.

If Elmer pointed out those trees, he felt sure that eventually, someone—probably that Puck boy—might take a hankering to try one of those berries, if they got hungry enough.

And that *wouldn't* be good.

He'd just keep the Holly trees to himself. Plenty of other uses for it, too.

Later.

For now, this concoction would work fine as a substitute in feeding their mental addiction of that first cup of hot brown tonic to start their day. Humans were creatures of habit. He could give this habit back to the ladies, and *that* would make them happy.

Probably.

He shrugged.

Hell, he didn't rightly know if'n it'd make them happy or not. After fifty years with his Edith, he still didn't know *what* made women happy. Fickle bunch, they were.

But it was worth a shot. He felt sure Grayson, Jake, and even Puck would thank him for that.

Jake squatted down and opened the sun oven door. He peered inside. "Nice set-up here, Elmer."

Elmer gave him a nod and sat down heavily in his lawn chair.

Jake stood up. "You know what would work even faster? A Fresnel lens."

Elmer nodded, but Grayson looked confused. "What's a Fresnel lens?"

"It's the lens out of an old flat-screen TV. You take the cover off the screen, and underneath there's a sheet of plastic in there—a lens—that magnifies sunlight to a fine-point beam. It'll light a 2x4 on fire in seconds. I've seen someone cook a two-pound roast and potatoes in three hours, using only two glass bowls and one of these lenses. We can do it even better using it with Elmer's sun oven. And you have the perfect TV down in your basement."

Jake had noticed the old TV years earlier when he'd helped Grayson move in. They'd struggled to get the old dinosaur down the narrow steps, into the small basement—which was more of a cellar—and Jake hadn't seen much use in doing it, since Grayson had told them the TV no longer worked.

He was glad now that they had.

"But how?" Grayson asked.

"Shoot a beam of sunlight through it onto that glass over the oven and it just works, man. Imagine a light saber from Star Wars," he explained. "You don't even need a lighter. As long as you have sun, you have fire."

"You don't say?"

"Yeah, man. You help me take apart that TV, give me some wood and screws to use for a frame, and we'll have one built in an hour—two tops. That is, if you can stand me tearing up your TV."

Grayson perked up. Nothing better than playing with fire... "*Pfft.* That tv ain't nothing more than a boat anchor at this point...and I'll do you one better. I'll tear it up myself. Let's go take a look at it. Here, hold my beer," he said to Olivia, handing her a wet dish-towel. "Let's git 'er done."

He and Jake hurried away, with Olivia rolling her eyes behind them, cringing at the sweaty towel she held up between two fingers.

4

TULLYMORE

THE MORNING SUN filtered into Tucker's bedroom, and he opened his eyes to find his arm slung over his wife's side. She was burning up and it wouldn't be long before she pushed it off. He watched the bedsheet—no longer damp—hang lifelessly in the open window, and prayed for a breeze. They'd hung it there to cool off the room.

Katie was still sleeping, a sheen of sweat on her face. If he wanted to make her really happy, he could get up, dip the sheet into the pool again and re-hang it, *just in case* a tiny wind blew through. If it didn't, she'd still appreciate his trying. But that would be wasting their rations of water, and with four teenagers, two dogs and themselves, they didn't have it to waste. Soon, they'd be up and working outside. In this heat, they'd need the water worse while working, than they would while sleeping.

Or so he thought.

It was possible Katie would disagree—she hated the heat. Summer without air conditioning in the South was truly an apocalyptic event all its own...not even taking into consideration everything else that was all wrong.

The country was in shambles, and Tullymore, the subdivision where Tucker and Katie lived with their four children, was running low on supplies. Tucker urged calm and took a proactive approach as their food stores dwindled lower and lower each day. For the half of the neighborhood that had voted him as leader, he assigned teams and tasks, such as foraging, gathering, and hunting, trying to stave off the panic.

Mostly his own.

Nearly everybody was just learning, but luckily, they had Neva, the neighborhood weird woman, who was instrumental in teaching them what plants and berries were edible around them, and how to harvest and cook it. They did their best to subsidize their food stores with what they could find in nature, and sent a team out to hunt each morning, but other than *one* rabbit, they'd yet to take down any meat bigger than a squirrel.

But they would, eventually.

Curt, who was the other leader in charge at Tullymore, led his group with a more lackadaisical approach. They ate when they wanted, and gorged on what was still in their pantries when the lights went off, with no regards for rationing, and no efforts to replenish it. They had finally started filtering the water in his own pool, after most of his group took ill, but the water level was nearing the bottom because they didn't ration; and it was still thick with sludge. They had no plan, and lived dangerously, day to day. More and more of that crowd had hungrily wandered over to Tucker's side, begging to be let in to his group.

He didn't deny a single one.

Instead, the soup was made thinner, the meat cut smaller, and the water stretched farther. He couldn't let anyone go hungry...but soon, he wouldn't have a choice.

He rolled over, already drifting back to sleep, hoping to prolong his reluctant duties of leader for just a few more moments.

As the sun continued to peek over the horizon, sending rays of sunlight down the quiet street lined with Dogwood trees, a small convoy of military trucks crept into the Tullymore subdivision, startling the crickets and the frogs into silence. The loud procession was led by a Humvee, and followed by two cargo trucks, their backs covered in green tarps.

A security team of four men posted at the entrance—shocked and surprised to see the trucks arrive—directed the convoy to Tucker's house. It was Xander's turn on watch, and he ran behind them as they crawled down the road, eyeballing the homes. He took a short-cut across the yards, beating them to Tucker's door, and hurried to get him as they parked, under careful scrutiny of sleepy-headed men stumbling to their porches, and women and children who were rousted from their beds by the unfamiliar sound of roaring turbo diesel engines rumbling in their 'hood once again.

Xander beat on the door with his fist. "Tucker! The army's here!"

Tucker emerged, still wiping the sleep from his eyes. "What?"

A stout man with an unfriendly face in fatigues walked up Tucker's driveway, meeting him with a stiff greeting. "You in charge here?" he asked. He squinted at Tucker past a scar that ran down his forehead, over one eye and halfway down his cheek.

Tucker blinked rapidly, looking past him to the handful of camouflaged-dressed men jumping out of the trucks with rifles slung over their shoulders. They met at the back of the middle vehicle, where they flipped the tarp up and stood silently on guard, the neighbors already gathering around them in curiosity.

"Yeah, I guess," Tucker answered, suddenly jolting awake, and peppering them with questions. "What is this? Are you National Guard? Are you here to help? What's going on? Do you have news of the grid? Is the power coming back on soon?"

The man with the scar held up his hand. A patch on his shirt announced his name as Cutter. "One question at a time please." He looked around at the waiting faces and leaned into Tucker, speaking low, "Can I come in, so we can speak in private?"

Tucker eyes slid down to Cutter's gun belt. He pulled his front door closed and stepped off the porch. "We can talk out here. Everybody will want to hear what you have to say."

The crowd quieted in anticipation.

Cutter's eyes narrowed, obviously not expecting or appreciating Tucker's refusal, and he and Tucker measured each other a moment.

Tucker straightened to his full height and waved the neighbors in closer.

Cutter took off his hat. "Okay. Fine. I'm with the Federal Emergency Management Agency. There's no news about the grid yet. But we brought food and water supplies."

The small crowd roared happily, but as Tucker looked closer at the trucks, he wished he'd paid more attention to the television newscasts after disasters. He couldn't remember what sort of trucks FEMA drove, but found it odd there were no identifying decals at all on the vehicles.

However, supplies were supplies.

They needed anything they could get. They'd been running very low on food and water, still having been unable to find a nearby water source and not comfortable travelling on foot too far from home.

"Thank you. We appreciate the help. But when will we know something—*anything*? Can you at least tell us what happened? Who turned out the lights? Was it Russia? North Korea? Terrorists? Is it just here the power went out, or everywhere?"

"That's still classified. My orders are only to bring food and supplies, and trade them out. Any other intel won't be coming from us."

Tucker raised his eyebrows. "Wait. *Trade?* Trade for what?"

"Guns." Cutter shrugged. "I've been given authority to trade one box of food supplies for every gun, and a gallon of water for every full box of ammunition. It's standard re-appropriation and distribution. The good guys need those guns."

5

TULLYMORE

TUCKER COULDN'T BELIEVE his ears. "We *are* the good guys."

Cutter scoffed. "I'm sure you mean well, but it'll be the men in uniform that brings civility back to the states."

"And you don't already have guns of your own?"

"Not enough, sir."

"So, this is a *gun grab*?"

"It's not a gun grab *yet*. Consider it a *Buy Back*. It's voluntary. You have no need for guns, sir. The government has this under control. You're safe out here, and we're making our way to every corner, from town to farmland. If *nobody* has a gun...well, other than us...then *everybody* is safer."

"Have you been *here*? Have you been to the *city*? I was nearly shot down by a gang of thugs *in the grocery store*. I've seen people killed—real people. Right before my eyes." A stab of fear knotted inside Tucker. What would these guys say if he admitted it was *them* that had done the killing? Were people now being brought up on charges? He still had nightmares about that gang standing behind him while he was on his knees in the deserted grocery store, a gun to his head. The memory of their lifeless eyes as they lay in puddles of their own lifeblood haunted him every night. It was kill or be killed, they'd had to do it...but would the authorities see it that way?

He hurried on, hoping to avoid any questions. "I haven't seen *the government* or a cop since the day the power went out. Or military—until you. And I don't imagine you're gonna stick around. It's the wild west out here and if the grid is not up soon, it's going to get worse."

"We're doing our best to secure your safety, sir."

Tucker scoffed, and looked carefully at his friends and neighbors—the crowd having tripled in the past moment as more came out to investigate and make their way over. He silently counted his blessings that he'd put off the conversation of *always having your gun on your side* that he'd been planning to have with the group.

There wasn't a gun to be seen on a civilian. So far, their little piece of earth had been mostly safe and unmolested. However, he was sure some of the men were carrying, but baggy T-shirts covered them well. He looked at his friends' faces, noting the smiles of relief now sliding away, and the small shake of their heads. They were in agreement with his thoughts.

Until the lights went back on and law was reestablished, they wouldn't relinquish their guns. They might be hungry and nearing desperation, but they weren't stupid.

He conspiratorially smiled at Cutter. "I understand." He held out empty hands. "Well, other than the few you saw with the security team up front, we don't have any guns here. We all lost them in a freak boating accident before the grid went down. Was hoping to replace them, when all of a sudden, all hell broke loose," he lied.

The man studied Tucker with a hard look. "Then you don't need food or water?"

"No, we *do* need it. Are you telling me you won't help us if we don't turn in some guns?"

The man nodded firmly. "That's my orders, sir."

The crowd bucked, turning back toward the men at the trucks.

"Give us some of that food!" a man roared.

"Please! My children need more to eat. They're hungry!" a bedraggled woman called out.

"Give us some clean water, at least!" Penny, the wife of Kenny, yelled.

The men jumped up on the back of the truck, sliding their rifles from their shoulders and pointing them at the crowd that was closing in on them. "Stay back!" one of the men yelled.

Tucker and Cutter rushed to the trucks, both yelling for everyone to calm down. Cutter pushed his way through the crowd and climbed up to speak. One of the other men handed him a mega phone and he spoke over the heads of the crowd, trying to reach the other people in the neighborhood, too.

"Attention! This is the Federal Emergency Management Agency. We're here to help. If you have a gun or ammo you'd like to trade for food or water, then bring it now. We'll stay here one hour."

Xander pushed his way to the front. "Respectfully, sir, we don't have what you're asking for, but we've paid our taxes. FEMA is supposed to be there for *all who are affected* in an emergency. We're *affected*. We're here, and we're hungry. You need to pass out some of that food and water."

Cutter ignored Xander and spoke again. "FEMA has appropriated a shelter in King's Mountain. It's a short drive and we've brought trucks for transport, with shade from the sun." He pointed at the tarps. "Food, water, medical care, shelter, *and protection* will be given for as long as needed, or until the power comes back on. Pack up any supplies you have, and load up within the hour."

"Where?" Tucker yelled over the crowd. "Where exactly in King's Mountain?"

Cutter put down the mega phone and answered Tucker, "It's a kid's summer camp. There's cabins, bathrooms, and everything anyone would need. Out on highway 321. Everyone welcome. Sir, we strongly encourage you to come with your group. We have plenty of food. We can protect you from these *thugs* you mentioned."

Tucker looked out over everyone. Something didn't feel right about this. He ran his hand through his shaggy hair. "I think I'll take my chances here, but I'll keep it in mind if things get too tough."

A murmur of agreement passed through the crowd and as one, they backed off the trucks, moving to stand behind Tucker, who wasn't the only one getting a bad vibe from this crew.

Cutter looked up to the sky, and breathed in deeply, letting it out in a heavy breath. He spoke to the whole crowd. "If you men aren't willing to come, we highly recommend you at least send your women and children... teenagers too. We *do* have guns. A lot of guns. We can protect them." He looked out over the crowd and laid eyes on the small group of teenagers that were standing together, including Tucker's four kids. "And for the older kids, who need more food, we've got everything from Pop Tarts to Doritos, to frozen pizzas."

Tucker's spine prickled at the man's obvious bribe.

"We've still got food, and we can protect our own," he answered for the crowd, receiving a tidal wave of heavy nods from everyone—other than the teenagers who looked at

Tucker with disappointment etched on their faces. "I think it's best we all stick together."

Cutter met Tucker's eyes and held a long stare, his lips squeezed into a thin line. "You're making a mistake. Bad things are coming. That's all I can say," he growled.

"Can't be worse than what's already came," Tucker replied evenly.

"You'd be surprised," he answered.

Tucker held his stare, not bothering to answer. The man jumped down. "Then we've got nothing else to say here. We'll make our rounds and be back through here in a week or so. I feel sure you'll change your mind by then. Good luck."

6

THE FARM

Bright and early the next day, Grayson and Jake were ready to tackle a new project.

Jake grabbed the front of the flat-screen TV, and eased it off, more than happy to see that on this one, the plastic protective cover that most people thought was the actual screen was only held on with Velcro. They wouldn't have to tear it apart. That would make it easier, and quicker. He quickly stripped that off and laid it against the wall, and then worked on removing the plastic sheet behind it.

First, he removed a mirror, carefully handing it to Grayson for safe-keeping, knowing Grayson liked to keep everything packed away in his barn or his container. Many times before, he'd thought of his brother-in-law as a pack-rat, or *Sanford the junk-man*, but he was seeing now that *less* wasn't in fact *more* when the stores were no longer open. *More* was more. They'd been using all manners of Grayson's junk since the lights went out, for all sorts of projects.

"Let's go," Jake said, carefully removing the Fresnel screen. It was a 32" TV, with the lens the same size. "See, it just looks like a big sheet of shiny, flimsy plexi-glass, but you have to be careful not to scratch it. It won't work right if you do—maybe not at all."

He duck-walked sideways up the steep wooden staircase, tightly gripping it in both hands, but not before taking a quick glance at the shelves holding a few dozen dusty Mason jars of food, four cases of bottled water, a porta potty, two plastic tote-containers marked 'sprinkler heads,' and 'patio cushions,' and another full shelf of toilet paper, paper towels and paper plates and cups. Another shelf held the few long-term food buckets he and Gabby had contributed, several blow-up mattresses deflated in their boxes were scattered around the floor, with a stack of bedding and pillows shrink-wrapped flat in plastic. On the very bottom shelf, there was a roll of plastic sheeting on top of a crate marked 'bio-haz.'

Grayson followed him up and answered his unspoken question. "Yes, that's more preps, but not a lot. And no, Olivia doesn't know they're here. She's refused to come down here since she moved in, for fear of spiders and snakes and stuff, and since she can lose more stuff than a leper on a pogo stick, I kept it to myself," he said and laughed. "Those plastic totes have some supplies in them. I just have them marked wrong in case anyone came snooping around."

"Any—"

"—no coffee," Grayson interrupted. "Sorry, pal."

The men moved to the barn, where they quickly made a frame for the plastic sheet, using wood cut down to one and a half inch by one and a half inch. They used three-inch nails for some overlap to secure it.

Once they had one side done, Jake put down two blocks of wood on the workbench in the middle of the frame and then lay the lens down on top of them, fitting it snug inside the frame.

Grayson watched. "What's the blocks of wood for?"

"That's just to stabilize it while we frame in the other side. We don't want the lens to bow up on us. It needs to lay perfectly flat," he explained.

They repeated the process for the other side and then cut a lip with same measurements, but smaller, going with quarter inch by quarter inch cedar. They mounted that to the frame, securing the lens flush in place.

They sat the lens aside, careful again not to scratch it, and then built a stand with eyebolts that they mounted it to. Jake tested it. It rotated perfectly.

They stood back and admired their work. The entire job took less than two hours.

"Looks like a big window," Grayson said. "Now what?"

Jake pulled his bandana off his head, and mopped his face with it.

Grayson looked at his brother-in-law with concern. "You feeling alright, Jake? It's not *that* hot in here..."

Jake nodded. "Yeah. I'm fine. Look, before we take this outside, you need to understand something. This thing is dangerous. And I do mean *dangerous*. You *cannot* leave it unattended when it's uncovered, and don't point it at anyone or anything that you don't want to see turned into a flaming ball of fire. You should never leave it out in the sun without first pointing the beam at something that won't catch fire, and even then, *never ever* walk away from it. Keep a dark sheet, or blanket or something to throw over it when we're not trying to cook something, or set something on fire, and you need to keep it put away in a dark place when we're not using it. But never, and I mean *ever*, leave it in your barn, or anywhere, without the cover. If the sun hits it, there's gonna be a beam, and something's gonna light up. You could burn the whole place down if you're not careful."

Grayson narrowed his eyes. "I don't even see a beam."

"Hold *my* beer," Jake said and threw his bandana at Grayson.

Grayson and Jake wasted an entire afternoon playing with the Fresnel lens. They lit fires, boiled water, and finally, experimented with cooking, using only a cookie sheet sitting on a sheet of metal that Grayson had dug out of his barn to cook eggs on, and then later with Elmer's solar oven, quickly cooking three jars of homemade butter bean and ham soup that Grayson had snuck out of the basement for a celebration.

For the first time since the grid went down, they were having fun, like two boys with a new toy.

They'd made cornbread with the lens, to go with their beans, and had laughed with glee when they unwrapped the aluminum foil insulation they'd used around the heavy Dutch oven, finding the top a bit burnt. They'd scraped it off and ate it anyway, dipping it into the hearty soup.

Grayson slapped Jake on the back. "This is so slicker than greased owl shit on a doorknob, bro," he said, as he watched Jake once again rotate the lens and point the beam, this time at a pot of chicory roots and water, heating it up to boiling in seconds for an after-dinner cup of 'coffee.'

"Jake, I gotta say, I know you weren't on the prepper band-wagon so much, but you're a hell of an asset to have around when the shit hits the fan. From making some gas usable, to using that scrap RV pump to get the women a real shower in the house, to all the other things you've done around here. Especially this... this is going to be a game-changer for cooking and starting fires. And it's a helluva toy, too. I'm glad you're here, brother."

Jake shrugged, humble as usual. "Yeah, thanks. But anyone could do this, really. Don't need me for it. Even Puck could start a fire or cook a meal with this beam. It's not rocket science."

Puck watched, peeking around from the corner of the barn, smiling widely at the big window-toy that Jake and Grayson were playing with.

Finally, he thought; something he could help out with, all by himself.

7

TULLYMORE

THE NEXT DAY at Tullymore began with Kenny reporting a huge problem to Tucker.

Kenny wrinkled his nose. "Well, the shit's hit the fan for real this time."

"Not the fan, but the floor, for sure." Tucker ran his hand over his face in frustration. "Why won't these people listen to anything? When the power went off, I *told* them to turn off their water and sewer valves. How hard could that be?"

"Some people are just plain stupid, man," Xander, the dark-skinned, American-borne Haitian replied, as he single-handedly loaded logs as big around as their waist into the back of a yard-wagon. He stopped and removed his doo-rag from his shiny black head and mopped the sweat off his face.

Tucker still found it strange to see Xander so casual, especially with a bandana on his head. He'd never seen the young entrepreneur in anything other than a full expensive suit before the grid went down. The man didn't even mow his own yard. He hired a team to come in every weekend to handle any outside maintenance.

Xander shoved the tip of the now-wet cloth into his back pocket and grabbed another log, slinging it on top of the pile with a huge crash, and a satisfying smile. "They probably thought it was a waste of time, thinking the power was coming back on any day now."

Tucker stomped off to pace and think a moment, and Kenny and Xander let him go. By now the three were thick as thieves, working shoulder to shoulder every day, and all three helping to guide the rest of the neighborhood.

Kenny started out being a pain in the ass, but was stepping up to be a huge asset, although Tucker and Xander had to teach him to do nearly everything, which took a good pit of patience from Tucker. But he was eager to learn, and gave it his all. The man they'd dismissed as a nerdy pencil pusher in the beginning was now an irreplaceable ally, worker, and friend.

Kenny's wife, Penny, had a propensity to stick her nose in, obnoxiously pushing Kenny on him for every project at every turn, and getting on Tucker's last nerve. Tucker and Katie assumed it had to do with the first day when Penny had nominated Kenny as the leader, and stubbornly stood as his only vote. She wanted him to be seen as important, somehow.

When Tucker had finally gave in to the nerdy man being in his shadow night and day, and embraced it instead of ignoring him, Penny had backed off.

Turned out they truly did just want to help.

Kenny took his self-appointed role as Tucker's sidekick seriously and he was used to dropping a problem on Tucker and then letting him work out the solution, or the plan, while hanging quietly by in wait, until Tucker gave him his marching orders.

Xander did the same. He had no need to be the boss—

he'd had enough of that in his nine-to-five before the grid went down. He was just glad to be home after his long trek back from the mountains of Tennessee, with his family in tow. The Carolina's had never looked so good, even though they rolled into it on barely more than a hope and a prayer, having crossed looters, robbers, and rapists on the way. He'd been happy to see his home still standing and untouched, and had been working hard every day since to help keep the 'hood afloat in this crisis.

Tucker scratched at his short beard and looked around.

The air reeked with the smell of raw sewage. Luckily, all the houses in their subdivision hadn't been affected yet. Only the ones on the lowest elevation in the 'hood, and only those who were on the *main* sewer line—so far.

Tucker groaned. He knew what the rest of his day would entail now; going house to house and handling the job of finding each water and sewer valve himself, to make sure they were all off.

This wouldn't fix the problem of some of their floors being covered in the stomach-flipping sweet smell of raw sewage, but it'd stop the entire neighborhood of being flooded with it. Tempers were on the verge of flaring due to food shortages, and hot, long work days without a shower or air-conditioned place to relax. The last thing he needed now was for their living conditions to get worse.

Yesterday morning, when they'd turned away the offer of the lopsided trade for food and water in return for their guns and ammo, Tucker had seemed to really wake up. It was almost as if he'd been in a fog, getting up each day and handling what the day brought, but not really planning for a long-term event; secretly hoping each day that *this* would be the day the power came on, or the government showed up with help and an explanation. He'd put off thinking about tomorrow, batting the thought away like a pesky fly.

But tomorrow was *here*. And whether he wanted it or not, he was the leader of at least half of these people, and he needed to start thinking like a leader; thinking long-term.

The neighborhood needed to be better fortified. The man in camo was right. Worse could come. Bad people were out there. He'd seen them up close—too close—and personal. A month ago, it looked like the whole town had been ransacked. Probably no food left for sure now. Soon, those bad people would be heading to the outskirts of town.

Places like Tullymore.

They'd need to be ready.

He had to find more water, too. The water in the pool was going down in huge increments every single day. It was less than a third full now, and every day they prayed for rain. It took a good bit of water for forty-ish people. Drinking, cooking, laundry, washing up... so many needs for water that no one really thought about until there was none, or not much.

There had to be another water source around here somewhere. They'd just have to find it—*before* they desperately needed it.

Food was another issue. They were quickly using everything they had.

Right now, the women insisted the men eat more, as they were handling the heavy outdoor work, most of the time. But the men insisted the women and children eat more; as that's just what good men did—took care of their families first. And the kids were demanding *they* get more, because dammit, they were *always* hungry and used to eating whenever they took the notion; especially the teenagers.

And the dogs.

Bottomless pits.

Both species.

The few dogs that survived Trunk's rampage through their neighborhood were now being fed mostly from their owner's plates. The day Tucker announced they could no longer spare extra food for those dogs was the day he really resented being the leader.

He loved dogs.

Especially his own.

Each evening he had to swallow down guilt that his own dogs, Hoss and Daisy, were secretly well taken care of, so far. They'd always kept two galvanized trash cans in the garage with extra bags of food. Wasn't really prepping—it was more of a convenience for Katie.

She enjoyed her grocery runs alone. In a house full of teenagers, alone-time was a rare gift. She actually looked forward to her weekly store run. But the dog food was too heavy for her, and took up too much real estate in the back of her SUV, room needed for enough food to feed a family of six.

So, Tucker took to stopping by once a month on his way home from work and buying half a dozen bags at a time and sticking them into the trash cans to rotate out.

The grid went down right after such a trip, so they were good for a while. He just wished the neighbors would've been doing the same. That was one thing Katie said she wouldn't share. She'd fight for Hoss and Daisy as though they were four-legged furry children.

To her, they were.

They were feeding them only once a day now, and late at night, one big bowl each, in the dark and away from prying eyes. He couldn't do it. Katie handled that. He couldn't stand those big brown eyes looking up at him when their one plate per day of food was gone. The dogs had always been fed twice a day before—morning and night—plus table scraps and treats.

Now *they* were on rations too, and looking a bit scrawny.

Meanwhile, the humans were still doing okay. But their belts were pulled a good bit tighter. Stoically, they were all mostly grinning and bearing it, as if this were one big glamping trip, without the glamour, and the wienies.

But *more* food wasn't happening for anyone anytime soon, and he knew the smiles and niceties would soon fade. People would get *real* hungry. And *real* mean. Mothers and fathers would do anything to feed their children if they were starving, and the 'hood would turn against each other. The food challenge seemed even bigger than the water. Surely, they could find some water, *somewhere*, and eventually the rain *would* come.

But food?

Food was going to be harder to come by.

Add extreme heat, and shit-water running through their houses, and things were gonna get crazy. Tucker returned to stand in front of Kenny and Xander. He sighed. "Send out the Town Criers, Kenny. Call a meeting for one hour from now."

While Tucker picked back up in helping Xander load the logs they'd cut, Kenny hurried off thru the gap in the houses and into the woods behind to round up the teenagers of the group. They had more energy and speed than the adults, and relished a chore such as this one. Much better than their never-ending job of cutting and gathering smaller firewood and dragging it back to camp, or even worse, the burning of the shit-barrels—which they'd complained about having to do.

Tucker smiled at the thought of their faces when he'd called them together in a special meeting early that morning. They'd been expecting a reward for all their hard work, and had stood tall with grins spread ear to ear, waiting. Unfortunately, he'd been given a report that they'd snuck out and were splashing around in the shallow pool the night before—their only source of water right now—so the *reward* was to assign them to the barrels, the *shit jobs*.

Their shit-eating grins had melted away real fast.

Even his own kids weren't exempt from some good hard work as punishment. All four were elbow deep in goo all day, with black-rimmed eyes from the smoke.

He felt sure they'd stay out of the pool from now on.

8

TULLYMORE

Around sixty people gathered in Tucker's backyard in the shade, under large rectangular beach canopies, and tarps strung haphazardly to trees and random sign-poles they'd dug up from the neighborhood, replanted in the ground for this purpose, as well as to hang clothes-lines on near the laundry area.

His numbers were growing. When the neighborhood first split, he and Curt each led around forty people each.

Now Tucker looked out at the crowd and saw that many of the faces that peered back at him were from Curt's group, marked by the tell-tale sign of them furtively glancing around looking for their own leader. Some of their faces were painted with guilt, other with defiance. Tucker didn't mind them hanging out for things like this. He wished the neighborhood wasn't split into two sides to begin with. They'd be stronger as one; and things were going from bad to worse for that group already.

Until they agreed to merge into one big group, and also shared some of their own food for the group pantry, he wouldn't allow them all to eat at the community supper. If they joined his group alone, though, he fed them with the understanding they'd be assigned to a work crew. But to convene for information purposes—or even to help out on security—was good for everyone. No one really gave them any trouble, as long as Curt wasn't there to instigate a problem.

And not surprisingly, Curt wasn't there. The last time Tucker had seen him was over an hour ago, laying in a hammock under a tree in his own back yard, sneakily snacking on something he kept hidden under his arm. He was neat and clean, as though taking a break from a long day behind the desk in his home office. Tucker was surprised he didn't have a few of the women standing over him, fanning him with big leaves, and feeding him as well.

The guy wasn't a leader. Lazing around, eating their food, while his people could be seen working wasn't setting a good example. Tucker looked at his own hands covered in callouses. His clothes were filthy; he wore a once-white T-shirt stained with who knew what, and torn-up jeans that now hung a bit looser on his lean frame, gathered together with his belt with a few new holes poked in it.

His boots had seen better days, too. His hair, which sorely needed cut *before* the grid went down, had grown over his ears and down his neck, just barely long enough to pull into a band at the nape, which his daughters pestered him into doing, and his sons laughed at him for.

He wasn't asking his own folks to do anything he wasn't willing to get out there and do himself, right beside them.

He shook his head in disgust at the thought of Curt lording over his new fiefdom, and then realized as he looked around that Sarah, his neighbor, was nowhere to be seen, either. He called his eldest son, Zach, over.

Zach hurried up from his seat on the ground, and

stretched his long legs as he stood in front of his father. He was more man than boy now, especially after the past few month's events. His light brown hair was now tipped in wild, golden curls from working out in the sun, instead of staying locked in his room on video games or his cell phone all the time. His arms were bulging with muscles, and Tucker was shocked to see he didn't need to look down to speak to him anymore. They were eye to eye now.

When did that happen? he thought.

"Take your brother and go check on Sarah, please. Tell her there's a meeting."

"I already did, Dad. She wouldn't open the door. She yelled through it and said she was busy with Sammi, and to go ahead without her."

Puzzled, Tucker scratched his now apocalyptic-beard. Not wanting to waste time, water, or the precious soap and shampoo he tried to save for his girls—he was out of shaving cream—he'd let it grow, and it was in the painfully-itchy stage. The group rarely called a meeting, but everyone knew if and when they did, it was usually *very* important. He was surprised that Sarah would miss it.

"Go over there again, son. Tell her she needs to be here to hear all this; I don't want to repeat myself. Unless her or the baby are sick or something."

Zach grimaced. "She *is* sick... or something. I can smell it through the door. It's a stench."

"Oh great. That means her house probably got flooded with sewage, too." But on second thought, Sarah's house shouldn't have flooded. She lived across the street from Tucker, and they were on the high side. No one else's house on their street had been affected yet.

He needed to get started with the meeting. They had a lot of ground to be covered, and then they needed to get back to work. He let it go and waved his son to sit down again. He'd have to make a trip over there himself, later.

Penny, Kenny's wife, overheard the conversation. "*Kenny* can run the meeting if you need to run over there, Tucker," she said, prodding her husband to stand up. "Go ahead, Kenny."

Kenny resisted, gently pushing her hand away and shushing her with a whisper, earning a cross look and pursed lips from his bossy wife, who then shot daggers from her eyes at Tucker, when he ignored her and turned back to the crowd.

Tucker knew Kenny well enough to know public speaking was *not* something he wanted to do. He cleared his throat. "Let's talk about the convoy. As most of you know, some guys in camo showed up willing to give us food in exchange for guns and ammo. *Our* guns and ammo. The crowd that was there at the time agreed with me. For anyone that wasn't present, they also told of a FEMA camp. You can wait for them to come back, or head out there on foot. It'll be dangerous, but we know exactly where it is. They made promises of plenty of food and water. To be fair, I wanted to make sure everybody knows about it."

He looked around at the faces staring back at him. None were surprised. He wasn't surprised that they weren't surprised. Without the modern amenities of television and music, the only means of entertainment now was gossip. The visit from the convoy would've spread like wildfire already.

None spoke up to disagree with the answer he'd given the convoy.

"Okay then. Next issue: as some of you are well aware, the sewage lines have backed up. We told you in the first meeting we had here to turn off your valves in the house, and on the street, if you had one. But some didn't listen. Now you're in a pickle, because there's not enough water to give you any extra to clean up the mess. We need it *all* for drinking, cooking and bathing."

Actually, he couldn't remember if it had been Jake or himself that had warned of this, but he knew it'd been said. He looked around at the guilty faces and felt sorry for them. With the stress of the grid down, and the lack of air-conditioning and water, the last thing people wanted to do was live with a shit smell, *or* pack up and move. But the choices were limited.

He continued. "We're moving into summer, and it looks like the power isn't coming back on anytime soon. It's gonna be hot and the smell will get worse... for y'all that have flooding, I'd suggest you double up on occupancy with a neighbor and wait it out. Maybe the smell won't be so bad once it dries up. Pack up and ask someone if you can stay with them. Many of us have spare bedrooms, or you can sleep on the floor."

Suddenly, the crowd perked up, and a wave of worried chatter moved through it. He realized what he'd said and tried to back up. "Look folks, I haven't heard *a word* about the power coming back on—or *not* coming back on. No one has heard a word about anything. We still don't know *why* it's off. We need to plan as if it's forever, just in case."

Tucker cringed at his last sentence, wishing he could take it back before it was even all the way out his mouth. *Damn this public speaking...* he wasn't made for it. His mouth was overriding his brain. The crowd roared, some at him, some at each other; panic rising over the words no one had wanted to say aloud. They'd all denied it in their minds, wanting to live in their own little bubbles and hope for the best. As long as they didn't say it out loud, it wasn't happening. They could keep hoping and wishing to wake up to the world moving at a regular pace again; air conditioning running, trucks on the road headed to stock the stores with food, flushable toilets and running water.

Tucker had just popped that bubble.

If the power *didn't* come back on, it would be life-changing. Not just for them, but for all of America. It would set them back a hundred years. It would be an *apocalyptic* event for sure; *hell, it nearly was already*, he thought, thinking back to his trip with Jake to the grocery store where five bodies now lay in their own pools of blood.

People would start dropping like flies, especially when they ran out of food and water. Many with serious health conditions would die from lack of medical care, or medicine running out—like the elderly lady in the wheelchair they'd found waiting for her kids to return, and giving up when she found out they would never come home again. She'd snipped her own oxygen tube as the last of her kin lay dead on the couch—having waited too long for more medication that couldn't be found.

There'd be fatalities from sickness too, without a constant source of clean water for the majority; maybe some here at Tullymore. Already there were rumors of some of Curt's people being sick with diarrhea and vomiting. Tucker felt sure it was the water in Curt's pool. Drinking it without properly filtering it was the epitome of reckless. If anything, he was *over*-filtering his own pool water for his group, but better safe than sorry.

With the continued absence of police and a working court of law, murder and mayhem on a large scale would erupt soon, taking lives at will. Even if Martial Law was declared, who would enforce it? Who would keep the bad guys off the streets and away from the law-abiding citizens?

No one.

That's who.

They'd be on their own. Just like they were now.

But he didn't need to tell the group all that. Right now, they needed to focus on what they *could* control, and leave the hand-wringing for later.

9

TULLYMORE

THE CROWD at Tullymore settled down once more, and Tucker continued. "Okay, listen up. The other topic on the agenda is keeping cool. Most of us have never lived without climate control. Many of us haven't ever had to work outside for long periods of time. And with our water situation, this heat is gonna be rough on everybody. We're going to have to tighten up on the water again soon, as well as the food rations. So, we need to be smart about the heat."

A low grumbling moved through the group at the mention of lowering rations again, but there's was nothing to be done about it. What they had on-hand wouldn't last long. Tucker ignored their disappointment.

"First, let's all try to stay inside, or in the shade, during the hottest part of the day, or a good portion of it. That's usually between 11 am and 5 pm. We'll avoid being in the sun during these hours, when we can. When you are working outside, cover your head to keep the sun off of it. Wear light-colored, loose-fitting clothes. Natural fabrics like cotton breathe better than synthetic fabrics like polyester, rayon, or lycra. If you do get overheated, a wet towel over your head or shoulders will help a lot—if you have the water. But staying hydrated is more important.

Sweating less is our goal, so that we'll not need to drink more water than we have to.

For inside the house, tune your windows. Strategically opening the right windows to get the best breeze in, and out again, is 'tuning windows.' Be sure to open some windows on the second floor, so that heat rising in the house doesn't build up. Then open some on the first floor, so that the hotter air leaving the second floor is replaced by the cooler air. On the first floor, choose windows that are toward the wind, so that the air *enters* more readily. On the second floor, choose windows on the lee, the downwind side of the house, so that the air *leaves* more easily.

You should also block the sun that comes through any other glass by closing the curtains and blinds, or covering with foil or other opaque material. Make-shift awnings outside, over any windows on the hottest side of the house, would help too, if you can rig something up. Stay in the cooler parts of your home. The north side will have a lower temperature than the south side. If you have a basement, hang out there. Rooms with carpet are hotter than rooms with hard floors, so stay in any rooms with flooring like concrete, laminate, or tile. Move your beds in there if you have to.

At night, try to use the cooler temperatures to cool down the house. Again, tune the windows *if* you have screens—if you *don't* have screens, you'll be at the mercy of the mosquitos, so choose wisely which you'd rather be: hot and sweaty, or hot and itchy."

Neva raised her hand and Tucker pointed at her. All eyes landed on the mysterious woman; some in a rude stare. She had her long, frizzy, black hair pulled up like most of the other ladies, probably trying to beat the heat, but was still wearing her signature big baggy shirt and long skirt, nearly covering her feet. Surprisingly though, she didn't look hot or sweaty, unlike nearly everyone there. The Carolina's in June could be brutal, and this one was no exception, but she looked cool as a cucumber.

In a deep, rumbly voice, she said, "If you have Vicks Vapor rub, you can smear a dab across your window sills that don't have screens. It'll help deter the skeeters. You can also pat a few dabs on your wrists, elbows and neck to keep them away when you're working outside. But don't use it if you don't have much—the medicinal uses of Vicks will be more important down the road."

"Thanks, Neva. Good advice," Tucker said, and continued speaking, "You can create a draft by opening windows across the house from each other, then trapping that cool air inside before the sun hits your house the next morning. Even five degrees will make a huge difference when the heat really ratchets up.

We shouldn't have many problems with this, but it needs to be said. If you'll avoid excess sugar, caffeine, or alcohol, it'll help you handle the heat better. Also, let your food cool down before eating it; fruits and fresh veggies are excellent and we'll be sending out a team to forage. Blueberries and plums should be in by now, and I know this area has a lot of them, if we can find them. Early tomatoes are up, and cucumbers and collards. May even find some wild radishes. Maybe we can barter with any landowners where we find anything. But don't eat hot foods if you can help it. The more your body has to work digesting a heavy meal, the more heat you are producing for yourself."

Tucker was hesitant to bring up gardens. He didn't want to bring everyone's attention to the fact their neighbors might be growing food when they'd run out of fresh veggies in the group pantry, using most of them to can stews and soups for later. That might be enough to start in-fighting or stealing. But this might be the last time they were all together for a while and he didn't have time to make one-one-one house calls to negotiate. "For those of you that might have your own little gardens..." He raised his eyebrows and looked around to see if anyone volunteered that information, or raised a hand.

He'd already seen four small gardens in the neighborhood, but no one had offered to share as of yet. Times weren't desperate enough to force that issue—for now—so he'd let them stand up voluntarily if they wanted to.

No one stood up.

Guess no one is ready to share.

"Be sure to save your seeds. Some may be heirloom and we'll need to replant those and see what comes up, or at the very least, sprout from them for some vitamin-something or the other." He wasn't sure how it worked, but he'd read something in a book that Katie had at the house about sprouts and the health benefits of eating those nasty weeds. He'd have to ask her to look into it for him.

"Moving on... be sure to cook *everything* outside—not indoors. Cooking inside is just going to add to the indoor temperature. We've still got some food for the group here and we'll continue to do the evening meal out here once a day, but we're gonna push it back an hour or so to get out of the heat."

Tucker looked off in the distance, trying to think of anything else he could add. Neva raised her hand again. He pointed at her to speak.

But instead of Neva speaking, her beautifully exotic niece, IdaBelle spoke this time. "Aunt Neva says if you have any Peppermint Essential Oil, sprinkle a few drops into your water when you wash up. It'll help cool you down too, or at least give you a cooling sensation."

A smart-ass in the back murmured just loud enough for everyone to hear, "I would if Tucker'd give us enough water to take a damn bath."

Another disembodied voice yelled out, "Can you show me how that washing up thing works, girlie? I'll gladly share my water with you."

Tucker—and IdaBelle—ignored the hecklers, and the entirely too long stares that many of the men gave her, with her full red lips, silky dark hair and curves. She was barely more than a girl—twenty-five, Katie had told him—and didn't court the attention on purpose. She was a natural beauty and probably couldn't hide it if she tried. She and her aunt, Neva, lived together.

He'd have to remember to keep an eye on them. Maybe he'd talk to Katie about moving them in with their family for a while, at least until when *and if* the power came back—which he knew in his heart of hearts wasn't happening. Better to take any temptation to make trouble away before it happened, then after.

He gave the girl a nod. "Thanks, IdaBelle. And Neva."

He looked around to see if anyone else was offering advice, but saw no other hands. He continued, "If we can locate another water source, or if we get some rain, we'll start wetting our clothes and wearing them damp when we work outside. We can re-soak them when they dry off. And if we find that water, we'll also be able to put a wet towel in front of the windows, or wet sheets in front of the doors, for the breeze to blow through. That'll cool the houses down a bit, too. I've even read where back in the days before air conditioning, folks would *sleep* in damp sheets. So that's a possibility down the road."

Tucker didn't *know* what to do about the water. The only water they had was in his and Curt's swimming pools, and Curt's looked nearly undrinkable by now due to his laziness. If it rained, the 'hood was ready with all sorts of make-shift water catchment set-ups: rain barrels, tarps in truck beds with downspouts pointed at them, and a row of kitchen containers lined every back porch to include pitchers, bowls and glasses of every size. But the rain had been absent, and his worry was growing. He planned to send a team out to look for a creek or stream again today in the nearby woods.

"For now, if you do get overheated, take care of it immediately. We don't want any heat strokes going on without medical care around here. Get a bandana or something else wet, and place it on your neck or other areas where your blood is close to the surface. Think pulse points–wrists, inner elbows, underarms, groin. Lay down in the shade, preferably where you can find a breeze. Hydrate the best you can, but don't waste water... we soon may need every drop we have, and more."

Tucker ended the meeting with a wave, and headed off at a fast walk, not wanting to be pulled aside by a dozen people with unanswerable questions right now. He didn't have all the answers. Hell, he barely had *any* answers. He was flying by the seat of his pants here.

The stress of being in charge was getting to him—and he had no idea his final words to the group would ring so true, so soon.

10

THE FARM

PUCK TWISTED a ring on his finger, 'round and 'round, as he paced the gun range where the women were busy, ten minutes deep into the woods, in a clearing where Grayson had his own homemade shooting range. Just a pile of dirt piled high and packed in with the tractor; plywood nailed up in front of it, and a thrown-together make-shift shooting table. They'd thrown a blanket on the ground for bystanders—or sitters, as the case was.

Tarra leaned back and stretched, and exchanged a harried glance with Tina, both barely concealing their frustration. She leaned over to whisper to her, "Stupid people are like glow sticks. I want to snap their necks and shake the shit outta them, until the light comes on."

Tina smothered a laugh as she once again stood to take her turn at giving Olivia instruction—Tarra's patience had run out. As she got up, she caught Gabby's disapproving stare; she'd heard them talking, and although she probably agreed, she didn't approve of the negative back-chatter about her twin sister. Tina gave her friend a guilty half-smile.

As usual, Tina began with a reminder of the range rules; including *cease fire* and *range is hot*, and then went over the five fundamentals of shooting: aiming, hold/grip control, breath control, trigger control and follow through. But an hour into the training, and Olivia still wasn't warming up to the idea of carrying a gun full-time; or comfortable enough with shooting in general to be relied upon when needed. Her movements were herky-jerky; her back hunched over, her posture tight and unyielding—but her wrists and hands were too loose.

The more she shot, the more she looked like Elmer Fudd on the range, all leaned over and *too* loosey-goosey with her gun, until she pulled the trigger, at which she'd jumped each time a bullet cracked air.

Jake had worked with Tarra alone, briefly, the evening before. She'd soon found out he already knew how to use a gun properly. He'd rather not mess with guns but he understood that now was not the time for rathers.

After only a short safety refresher and a few minutes of shooting, Tarra had put an end to the training session with Jake. No use wasting bullets. He hadn't needed more training, it had all come back to him. He'd just needed to shoot a few times to practice, and to carry and handle his gun at all times to get used to the feel of it.

They'd gone through more ammo than they should have in the first half hour with Puck, too, and soon sent him to the blanket with a pat on the back and declaration of trained, seemingly sad to be made to stop wasting lead.

Puck was a joy to teach. All big eyes and open ears, soaking in every bit of instruction. He was eager to please everyone, especially *GrayMan*, as he called him. The boy was a natural, which didn't surprise the group at all. After finding out he'd exceled at sports before his head injury, and seeing him in action with Trunk and his gang, they didn't expect any less from him. He'd been reluctant to stop shooting, as he enjoyed it so much. Now, he was like a jack in the box, popping up and off the blanket every few minutes; restless and unable to sit still.

Graysie and Gabby had been excused from training by Grayson. He'd taught Graysie himself, and had broken lead with Gabby many times. They were just here to watch.

Olivia's training was another story.

"Cease fire!" Tina yelled loudly.

Olivia set the gun down, pointing it down-range and stepped back from it.

Tina stepped up to coach her once again. "You need to loosen up a bit just before, and after, you pull the trigger."

Puck sidled up to the women, Ozzie at his feet. "Can Olivia be done now?" he whined.

Tina gave the boy a look. "No. You had your turn, Puck. Go sit down."

"I don't want another turn. I want Olivia to be done."

Olivia smiled at Puck. "It's okay, Puck. I need Tina or Tarra to tell Grayson I can outshoot Annie Oakley, so I'll keep trying until I do." She gave Tina and Tarra a snarky smile, and then as Puck hung his head and walked away, she attempted to loosen up.

Graysie patted the blanket. "Puck, you and Ozzie come over here with me." Puck hung his head as he went to sit between Gabby and Graysie, and Ozzie squeezed his way in, nudging his ball to Puck, in hopes he'd throw it. Puck ignored him, his pout completely lost on the dog.

Tarra leaned back from her spot at the end of the blanket and tossed grass on Puck—not even earning a smile at her attempt to cheer him.

He only had eyes for Olivia right now.

Olivia took a deep breath, and stepped back to the table, announcing, "Range is hot," as she'd been taught, and picked up her gun. She took her stance, squeezed her eyes tight and jerked the trigger, jumping once again at the sound she knew full well was coming.

Tina cringed. "Cease fire! Stovepipe," she announced loudly. She hurried toward Olivia, who lowered her gun to low ready position. "Finger off the trigger! Put your gun down and back away."

Olivia safely laid her gun down and stepped back. "Cease fire," she repeated quietly to herself.

Tina took the gun, popped the magazine out, racked the slide to open the action, and removed the casing. "A stovepipe happens when a spent casing fails to eject correctly. That causes the casing to get trapped upright in the slide."

She checked the action and the barrel to be sure there were no other problems—it appeared there were not—so she left the action open and laid the gun down again. "Check it and chamber," she instructed Olivia. "Range is hot," she announced loudly.

Olivia picked it up, pointing it in a safe direction, and stepped up to the shooting line. She released the slide release lever to close the action, and made sure the hammer was up, and re-loaded her magazine. She racked it, realigned, and pulled the trigger, jerking as though still surprised at the crack of the bullet.

Puck jumped up once again, hurrying over to pull at Olivia's arm, with Ozzie behind him. "Come on, Olivia," he whined. "I want to *show* you something right *now.*" He was nearly vibrating with impatience, like a toddler who wanted his mother's attention and wanted it *now*.

Olivia turned to look at the boy, having to look up to do

it as he towered over her, and firmly pushed him away. "Puck, no. Go sit down now, and be still. Tina said *range is hot*. When someone says that, you don't go near them or move around, and you *especially* don't touch their arm if they're holding a gun. You could get shot."

"So could you," Puck mumbled and walked away, his head hung low.

Ozzie loped hopefully behind him, with his ever-present tennis ball dripping from his mouth.

Olivia stepped up and once again struggled with the slide. She heaved a big sigh, looking to her sister, Gabby, for help. She just wanted this *over*. But she'd promised Grayson she'd keep trying until the ladies declared her trained and ready.

Gabby caught her glance and a pang of guilt hit her. Olivia *was* trying. This didn't come easy to her. It would be like Gabby trying to clean and dress a wound. They each had their skills and guns weren't Olivia's. She had to help her, no matter how frustrated she was with her sister about so many things, and no matter how many times she'd already tried to teach her, with her own instruction falling on deaf ears.

But *sisters* stuck together.

"Wait." Gabby hurried to the table and took the gun. "Olivia, I have trouble pulling back slides, too. Here's a trick I learned. Don't pull back the slide like most people do. Hold the slide firmly in your left hand, but push the gun away from you with your right hand, then release it quickly. It accomplishes the same thing." She demonstrated without actually chambering it, only mocking the movement, and then laid the gun on the table and stepped back a few paces. "And don't jerk the trigger. *Easy* on the trigger, cowgirl..."

Tina nodded her approval and stepped back with

Gabby, out of the line of fire, announcing, "Range is hot," in a bored voice.

Puck jumped up once again, nearly tripping on Ozzie. "Wait! Let's do something else now. I'm bored!" he wailed, his face turning red. "Let's go right now."

Olivia turned, putting her hands on her hips. "Puck! What is wrong with you? You had your turn, now it's my turn. Go run along and find something else to do. We're staying here until I get this right," she scolded him in a firm voice, finishing with a long look that brooked no argument.

She blew out a breath of frustration at his constant interruptions and stepped up to the table. "Range is hot!" she said, and stiffened up yet again, squinted her eyes, and squeezed the trigger, and then looked down at the gun in disappointment. The bullet casing was sticking out of the top.

Another stovepipe.

Olivia shook out her arms with a ridiculous gesture similar to shaking wet noodles, expecting someone to admonish her once again to loosen up.

She was still holding the gun.

Tina cringed. "*Range still hot*!" Defeat was showing in her own shoulders now. "Olivia, I meant put the gun down first, and *then* loosen up your body. *Not* your arms and hands. You're already limp-wristing it. That's what is causing those stovepipes. You need a better grip on the gun. Tighter. And, you're still anticipating too much and jerking the trigger. Take a deep breath through your nose, and let it out your mouth. This doesn't have to be stressful. Shooting can be fun!" she said with a fake smile plastered on her face, clearly about to lose her cool with Olivia, too.

Puck paced behind the ladies, his hands on his head,

stealing glances toward the shooting table at every pass. The boy was seriously anxious.

Olivia placed the gun on the table and stepped back. "Cease fire," she muttered and followed direction, putting her body through a flurry of adjustments, trying to keep up with Tina's demands. Finally, she took a deep breath, picked up her gun, and tried to relax. "Like this?" she asked, looking at Tina for approval.

"Range is hot!" Tina reminded her loudly, and then nodded, whether out of agreement or resignation, it wasn't clear. "Looks better. You went from leaning too far forward, to starting to lean backward, like your gun was going to turn around and chase you. Looks good now."

Olivia paused to beam at Tina's reluctant approval and turned to give Gabby a smug smile. The twins had argued earlier over the 'teacup' grip, and Olivia had slid it in without Tina correcting her. Taking any win she could get against her sister, she bobbed her head. "See that, Gabby? Tina didn't mention my tea-cupping."

She pointed the gun downrange and pulled the trigger.

Click.

The gun didn't fire.

"Range is hot," Olivia announced loudly in a frustrated voice, and placed the gun on the table, looking over her shoulder for Tina to help her.

Tina's face was impassive. She took a deep breath, looking at the sky as she let it out slowly.

Gabby stood up and Puck jumped to his feet like pop goes the weasel. She waved him to sit down and stepped toward the range. "I got it this time, Tina. Sit down and take a break." She hurried to her sister's side, reaching for the gun, when—

boom.

11

THE FARM

GRAYSIE AND GABBY screamed in unison at the fountain of crimson coming out of Puck's hand, while Puck stared wide-eyed at Gabby, and then the entire group fell silent.

The air filled with a tangy, coppery smell, as the screaming stump raised red ruin.

"Omigod, Omigod, *Omigod...*" Graysie chanted, jumping to her feet and running toward the table. Ozzie let loose a flurry of frantic barks, backing up on his haunches with his nose in the air. Tina and Tarra jumped up. The women surrounded Puck.

In seconds, Puck had shadowed behind Gabby and had forcefully shoved his arm in front of her, to block her hand from picking up the offending gun, just before it went off.

Olivia and Gabby both stood open-mouthed, staring at Puck's hand.

Gabby exhaled. "Let's get you home, buddy."

Olivia jumped into action, issuing orders. "There's no time. And he might pass out. We can't carry him. Hurry, Gabby. Hand me the range bag." She pointed to the black zippered bag.

As Gabby scrambled for the range bag that Grayson insisted be present at the shooting range at all times, Tina slowly closed her eyes and shook her head. "Shit," she muttered. She turned around and ran for the blanket.

Tarra pursed her lips, staring at Puck's hand. "Olivia, what have you done?" There was an edge of anger in her voice. She gripped Puck's wrist firmly with a grimace, raising it in the air, higher than his heart.

Olivia rapidly shook her head. "I didn't do it! Just shut up! Let's focus on Puck!"

Tina quickly spread the blanket out on the ground. "Sit down, Puck."

Puck sat down heavily, still holding his hand in front of his face, with Tarra quickly squatting beside him, her hand still firmly in place around his wrist.

"We've got to stop the bleeding," Olivia said as she dug into the bag. "We can't even see the damage until we do that."

Puck's chin quivered. His entire hand, and now wrist to the elbow was painted a solid crimson color. "It's gone, Olivia. GrayMan is gonna be mad at me."

Olivia spared him a quick glance, and then went back to opening zippers, trying to find the Israeli compression bandage she knew had to be in there. "What? What's gone?"

"*GrayMan's* ring. He gave it to me today," he screamed. "He said since I didn't get one. He finished school. And then they gave him a ring," he explained in a lower voice, in the funny way that he talked. He leaned forward, squinting to try to see through the tsunami of red blood pouring out.

Tarra gripped his arm tighter. "Puck, hold still. Don't worry about a stupid ring."

"It's not stupid!" Puck blew air out his nose. His face was getting pale.

Grayson had gifted Puck his high school class ring that very morning, having come across it while looking for his spare holsters. Puck had been proud to wear it and could barely take his eyes off of it all day.

Olivia found the First Aid Kit and popped it open, jerked out the Israeli compression bandage and ripped the package open with her teeth.

"Omigod," Graysie squealed, her hands over her mouth. She paced back and forth.

Oliva shot her a stern look. "Graysie, get it together. You'll scare Puck. It's not that bad," she lied, sending Graysie a conspiratorial wink.

Graysie swallowed hard. She closed her eyes and stood stock-still for a moment. Exhaling as she opened them back up, she stood behind Puck and patted him on the shoulder. "Yeah. It's… it's going to be okay."

Puck tilted his head to look straight up at Graysie. His innocent eyes were filled with tears. He nodded, not as if he agreed, but slowly as though pleading with her to convince him, and make it so.

"Yeah," Graysie answered his beseeching look. "You'll be throwing the ball for Ozzie in a day or so. Probably." She pasted a weak smile onto her face.

Olivia pulled the bandage from its outer pack, then ripped open the inner packaging and slipped the bandage out. She looked hard at it, pulling on the end and studying it, then looking to Puck's hand again. "Dammit! This won't work. It looks like the blood is coming from one of his fingers. I can't wrap that with this big thing." She dived back into the kit and pulled out a package of QuickClot bandages. She ripped it open, taking one white roll out.

Tarra snatched up the Israeli bandage with her free

hand. "Can't we wrap it around his wrist? Wouldn't that help slow the flow of blood?"

Olivia shook her head and scooped up a bottle of water, then scooted over to Puck and Tarra with the smaller Quick-Clot bandage. "No, let's just use this. Lower his hand down to me, Tarra. And Graysie, I need *you* to run as fast as you can and get the surgical kit. Hurry!"

Tarra kept her grip, but gently lowered Puck's hand toward Olivia's lap.

"I can't *feel* anything," Puck whined, staring at his hand.

"Good. We get this done fast enough and you may not feel a thing until it's over. Now, I need you to not look at it anymore, okay? Look at Ozzie. See how much he loves you? Just watch him." Ozzie had planted his head across Puck's ankle, giving little whines of concern, and staring up at Puck with big, soulful brown eyes.

Olivia poured the water onto Puck's hand and eyeballed the wound for just a second before a curtain of blood concealed it once again.

She and Tarra locked eyes.

This was bad.

Tarra bit her lip and exchanged glances with Tina. Her face showed she too had gotten a good look in the split second they could actually see anything.

Tina scooted in close and caught Puck's attention while Olivia jerked her head to Gabby to lean in. She whispered into her ear, "Run fast to the house. Make sure Graysie brings Grayson back with her. Tell Grayson I'm trying to stop the bleeding and to come quick, and that he might need the *thing* he used on the deer last season to separate the bones."

Gabby cringed and jumped to her feet, taking off in flight behind Graysie.

Olivia pushed the unrolled QuickClot bandage onto the wound and held it very tight, praying that her husband would hurry and take over this horrific job for her.

Puck jolted, startling both Tarra and Olivia.

"Hold still!" they both said in unison.

Puck pointed with his right hand. "Bacon Bit!"

The women turned to see Bacon Bit, the pig—still clad in a bedraggled, tattered purple tutu—nosing the ground on a particularly bloody spot of grass, not at all where Puck had been standing when he was shot.

Olivia waved a hand at her. "*Shoo!*"

Bacon Bit was moving fast, its flat nose as red as Rudolph's, pushing through the grass, grunting and nosing like a blood hound on the trail of a sweaty rabbit.

Puck screamed in alarm. "There's the ring! That's Gray-Man's ring! No, Bacon Bit!"

Olivia, Tina and Tarra all gasped as Bacon Bit grabbed the ring—and all that it was attached to—and ran.

12

THE FARM

GRAYSON STRUGGLED up the last few steps of the porch, his burden heavier than he himself was. Puck was in his arms. He was followed by the ladies, and a trail of blood that slowly dripped from a paracord-wrapped stub, pulled tight as a tourniquet.

Plop, plop, plop

The bullet had taken the finger off between the hand and the first knuckle, leaving just enough to wrap it twice; long enough to carry him to the house.

The boy had finally passed out, thankfully.

When Graysie had ran up to Grayson, skidding to a stop with eyes full of panic, his heart had nearly stopped. He'd thought something was wrong with Olivia. When she'd told him no, it was *Puck* and that he'd been shot—again—his heart did stop. It was a long moment before he could breathe or even move. He'd stared at Graysie, trying to make sense of her words, as she'd bent over, her hands on her knees, trying to catch her breath.

Gabby had shown up then and told him Puck was alive,

but that Olivia had sent for him, and told him to bring a bone saw.

But, if it was *that* bad, they needed a cleaner working environment than the ground. He'd given Graysie and Gabby instructions on preparing a clean area in the house, and told Jake what tool he needed and reminded him the quickest way to sanitize it, and then had ran to Puck.

Now, as he gently lay Puck down on the bed, he took a deep breath. He needed to stay calm. He needed to *be the calm*, even though it felt like this was his own oversized man-child laying there bloody and nearly lifeless. He had to walk Olivia through this, and it was going to be difficult for her.

He could do it himself, but he wanted—*needed*—to know the women could also do this if something should happen to him, or if he wasn't around. Olivia was the best bet. She seemed to find her calm in the middle of a medical crisis, and had more knowledge about basic first aid than any of the other women; maybe even himself. She'd already handled patching up Puck from the first gunshot wound he'd received from Graysie, without blinking an eye.

Grayson cringed.

Poor kid. That had to hurt worse than a splinter in the dick.

Then she'd taken care of removing dozens upon dozens of bee stingers and treating the stings on both Puck and the dog, Ozzie.

He shook his head.

We're bad luck for Puck. Either that, or this kid could screw up a one-car funeral.

Grayson grimly pulled on a set of latex gloves, matching the ones his wife wore. "Let's get started."

Olivia blew out a deep breath and swallowed hard, then grit her teeth and hoped Puck would stay out. What she'd been doing the past five minutes—without local anesthesia—would have brought even the strongest man to his knees. "I think this is the last of it."

Puck's hand lay lifeless on the make-shift surgical table —a rolling cart covered with a clean sheet that was once white. The last tiny shard of bone made a *clink* sound as it hit the bottom of the glass bowl. With a sigh, she placed the tweezers on the sheet with the other surgical tools. It hadn't taken long to debride the wound, after they'd cleaned it, and now they were ready to clean it again with the sterilized saline, and suture it closed.

She swallowed hard again, trying to keep her lunch down. She looked up at Grayson.

He nodded firmly. "You can do this. Keep going. Just pretend that you're sewing up the finger of a glove."

She took a deep breath and dove in, her face frozen in horror as she desperately tried to work the sagging pieces of thin flesh up on his ring finger. The *meat* was gone, leaving a pointy white bone pointed straight up out of the baggy skin puddled around it.

She curled her lips, feeling the nausea creep up her belly. "Be ready to help me hold the skin closed so I can sew it," she murmured to her husband, her eyes on Puck's stump of a finger.

Olivia looked up at Grayson with panicked eyes, her hands shaking. "There's not enough...*skin*," she whispered, her voice almost frantic. "The bone is still sticking out the top."

Graysie, standing on his other side of Puck, and gently holding his good hand while holding back her tears, flipped her curly long red hair over her shoulder and stared at the wall with a quiet sob. Gabby, standing behind her, rubbed her back in small circles.

Grayson walked to the door. "Jake, Elmer, Tarra, Tina... I need all of you in here."

Jake entered the room, followed by Elmer and the ladies, all with grim faces. They already knew what Grayson needed. He had briefed them all on the *what-if*.

They gathered around the bed, the men standing at Puck's shoulders, the women near his feet. They were ready to put their hands on him, to hold him down with their weight if he should fight it.

Olivia stared at her husband with pleading eyes. "Wait! Can't we just do the best we can and stitch around the bone?"

"No. That'll leave it wide open for infection. It's either now or later, and now will hurt less." Grayson looked around at the morose faces. "Y'all ready? I'll try this, but if the bone splinters...well, I don't know what we'll do. If he wakes up you may have to hold him down. Olivia, when the bone is out of the way, be ready to go at it again—fast—with saline to irrigate it, then jump in with the tweezers if there's any bone fragments, and then sew it up quick. Leave the end stitches open to allow drainage. We'll bandage the tip with sanitized wet gauze. Everybody on three..."

A shiver ran through Olivia and she stepped back to wait, her hands in the air to keep her gloves sterile. Tears rolled down her face. She could barely stand to look.

Grayson picked up the bone saw and leaned in. Puck's eyes popped open just as Grayson picked up his hand, folding the four intact fingers down and holding them there with a tight grip. The boy smiled. "GrayMan..." he said weakly.

Grayson tried to hide the saw, lowering it and sliding it behind his back, but it was too late. Puck had seen it.

His weak smile quickly slipped away. He moaned, his eyes filling with questions. "GrayMan? What—"

"—*Shhh*... I won't lie to you. This is gonna hurt worse than screwin' that bees nest, kid. One. Two. Three..."

The group all leaned over, laying a small army of tortured hands on Puck.

13

TULLYMORE

TUCKER AND KATIE stood outside Sarah's door. After not showing up to the meeting the day before, and sending their son away, Katie was adamant she wanted to bring Sarah some food and check on her today.

Tucker felt terrible he hadn't made it over yesterday, but he'd been pulled in too many directions, both during and after the meeting, and had nearly crawled into bed, exhausted last night.

Katie looked to her husband and sniffed, her face painted with disgust. She pulled the bandana tied around her neck up over her nose. Their son had been right. The smell was revolting.

Tucker knocked on the door.

There was no answer.

"Sarah?" Katie called out.

Tucker stood just behind Katie, waiting with his hands on his hips. He didn't mean to be impatient, but he had work to do. It was soon to be after noon, and he'd spent the first half of the day splitting firewood. Through the grapevine, he'd been told the entire neighborhood was out of propane for their grills, and if anything was going to get cooked—for anyone—it would be over an open fire from now on, and that was going to take *a lot* of logs.

The faster he could get Sarah squared away, and her and the baby out of that house, the faster he could get back to it.

He also planned to try his hand at cooking rabbit stew in a haybox today. The minutes were flying by. Not enough time in the day to handle every crisis.

Wow. That smell is almost overwhelming.

He couldn't understand why Sarah's house had sewage back-up. His didn't. And it was on even lower elevation, across the street. No one on this street had reported their toilets backing up, and he'd checked with each of them. But Sarah's was *ripe*… if he could smell it through the door.

Tucker rapped on the door again. "How long has it been since you talked to Sarah?"

Katie shrugged. "A week? I don't know. I see so many people come and go getting their water rations from the pool, or eating supper, that I can't keep up with which days I see who anymore. She's been over to eat when Sammi's napping, usually, if she comes at all." She turned back toward the door. "And I'm not out there all the time either. I've got plenty of other things that keep me busy."

"She's got to be getting the rice-water for Sammi every day though," he muttered, mostly to himself, trying to remember if he'd seen her at the house. "And water for herself, not to mention the extra water I told her she could have to wash Sammi's cloth diapers."

He sighed and stepped past his wife, knocking louder than she had. They couldn't leave Sarah and the baby in this stink. Her husband had been deployed before the grid went down, and Sarah was having a tough-go handling a newborn—Sammi—alone, especially with the power out *and* having run out of formula, and then the baby getting so sick.

Neva's suggestion of giving the baby rice water had seemed to be a last-minute miracle; Sammi had very nearly died of starvation and dehydration. The rice water was packed with nutrients, and that had worked to nourish the baby back to health, although no one had seen her since her recovery.

Sarah was too afraid of germs getting to her and causing her to get sick again.

But with this situation, she was going to have to risk the germs, and stay with him and Katie and the kids. If Neva and her niece came too, it was going to be a full house. "Sarah, wake up! You and Sammi can come stay with us until we figure out a way to clean up the mess."

Finally, they heard a rustling in the house. A moment later, Sarah cracked open the door. The smell hit them like a wall, and Katie backed up, nearly falling off the top step. He caught her and pulled her upright, then pulled up his dirty wet T-shirt to cover his own nose.

Sarah stared at them through bloodshot eyes buried in dark circles, seemingly unaffected by the smell. For a moment, Tucker wondered if the smell was *her*, she looked so bad. Her clothes appeared to have been worn and slept in for days, and her hair hung loose in ratted-up clumps. She was so thin, her clothes hung from her hunched-over bony shoulders.

Even in a grid-down situation, the ladies were still brushing their hair, usually pulling it up to beat the heat, and attempting to look somewhat clean and put together, at least to *start* their day. By the end of the day, there weren't many who didn't look bedraggled.

But Katie was *far* from put together.

"You okay?" Tucker asked her.

Sarah's eyes were cloudy and droopy. "Yeah, fine. Why?"

"You don't look so good," Tucker answered. "You look sick. Have you been getting drinking water from Curt's pool? We haven't seen you at the house much."

She didn't respond. She just stood staring at Tucker. Katie stepped around him, holding her bandana over her nose. "Sarah, do you need some help with Sammi? If you're sick, I can take her and let you get some time to yourself. You can clean-up or rest... actually, Tucker and I came over to tell you to come stay with us. If your house was hit with the sewage flood, you and Sammi can't stay here," she said in a muffled voice.

Sarah was shutting the door even as she spoke. "No, we're fine. We're staying here—" The door firmly shut, and the deadbolt clicked in place.

"—Sarah, you *can't* stay in that stink," Tucker said through the door, and ran his hands over his face. "It can't be good for the baby! Open the door."

He and Katie exchanged looks and Katie shrugged. "Let her be, Tucker. You can't force her out. If she wants to stay, she can stay. It's her home. She might just be too tired to make the move; she looks like we woke her up from a nap. We'll let her rest and then I'll come back and—"

"—Tucker! The pool! It's draining!" Kenny yelled from across the street, waving his skinny arms frantically. "How do I make it stop? We're losing water!"

Tucker froze with a look of panic, and then ran, as fast as he could in heavy boots, back to his own yard. He slid around the corner of the house, slipping in a smear of mud.

Holy shit!

Mud?

It hadn't rained since before the grid went down.

He picked himself up and limped to the back yard as fast as he could.

It only took a second to see the problem, even through the disorganized mess of chairs, tables, nets, and other things littering the patio. He stomped over to the corner of the pool, reached in, and pulled out the dirty green water hose that stuck out like a green thumb.

"Who put this hose in here?" He looked around, furious. The two ladies at the laundry station nearby returned a look of bafflement.

The children in the yard stopped playing and shrugged with wide-eyed innocence.

Two men carrying a load of firewood to the cook pots shook their heads.

No one saw anything?

Someone had put it in there to siphon the water out. It didn't fall in there all by itself.

He followed the hose as it wove between their filter systems on the concrete around the pool—the whole filtering set-up pushed up closer to camouflage it—off the concrete and into the grass, where it drained going down a slight incline, making mud in a fifty-foot trail.

Along the muddy trail were footprints of a man's boots. Not a real large foot, maybe a size eight or nine. Possibly a teenager. The kids had been playing in the pool a few nights before, but the hose should've been noticed by now. Maybe they'd snuck in again last night? And *why* would they put a hose in there?

No, it would've been drained by morning if they'd put it in last night. This had to have been done *today*.

"How the hell does someone stick a hose in a pool without being *seen*?"

More heads shook.

He had everyone's attention now. "You all just let it happen? Do you not realize how important this water is? Do you *not* understand this is all we have? That we'll die without water? Are you *awake* yet? This is NOT A DRILL, PEOPLE. The lights are out for good! The water isn't coming back on! *No one* is coming to help us. We needed every damn drop... *and more*!" he roared, not able to contain himself anymore. This was the straw that broke the camel's back.

It was *too* much. He was over his head. He couldn't be the person responsible for all these people. He had his own family to worry about. *Why am I even doing this?*

He threw the end of the hose down, slamming it onto the ground as hard as he could, and precious water splashed back up at him. He turned, eyes full of fire and stared at the pool, now at least a few feet shallower than it was when he'd left that morning. He paced, his fingers weaved together on top of his head, and then whipped around, looking for a target for his anger.

Kenny.

"You didn't see this *hose*, Kenny?"

Kenny adjusted his thick glasses and fidgeted, looking at the ground. "No... I'm... sorry. I didn't even look before coming to get you. I thought...I thought... maybe a valve was turned on or, or... something... I don't know anything about pools, Tucker," he stuttered.

"Do you know *anything* about *anything*?!" Tucker yelled. "I can't watch everything, plan everything, and *do* everything around here! What use *are* you? Grow some balls, Kenny!" He stomped off into the house to cool down just as Katie ran around the corner, seeing her husband in melt-down at Kenny.

Kenny's wife, Penny, was standing off to the side,

hunched over with her arms crossed, glaring at Tucker with daggers in her eyes. Katie couldn't blame her. No one liked to see their partner embarrassed.

Katie hurried by and squeezed Kenny's arm. "He didn't mean it. He's just overwhelmed. He told me just today he's glad he has you, and you've been a huge help," she lied, and then followed Tucker into the house.

14

TULLYMORE

ALL DAY KATIE had kept an eye out for Sarah, hoping to see her show up feeling better. She planned to extend the invitation to stay with her and Tucker again, and had hoped Sarah would come there, instead of Katie having to brave the smell once more.

After leaving Sarah's house, and dealing with the pool draining—losing half of the water they'd had—it'd taken hours to get that funky smell out of her nose. She'd finally resorted to washing up mid-day, feeling like the funk was *on* her, and sneaking while she scrubbed her face and neck and arms, as that'd be seen as wasting water.

It *was* her and Tucker's pool, after all, thus by all rights it was *their* water. But they didn't want to pull that card and take more than they were allowing everyone else, especially now that the water level was even lower. That's not the type of people they were. Instead, she'd just skip washing up this evening to make up for her mid-day scrub.

Sarah hadn't shown up, and Katie felt like she couldn't just leave her there without supplies, and without offering the invitation one more time. She had to go back.

She stepped through her yard and looked up into the evening sky. It was filled with twinkling stars. *Beautiful.* Either she hadn't taken the time to really look lately, or they really were shining more than usual. Maybe with the power out and no exhaust fumes in the air, the sky was different, opening up to show them the wonders they'd been missing in their busy rat-race world.

She drew in a huge breath of night air.

And gagged, sputtering it back out again.

The smell.

It was now out as far as the road.

It was as though Sarah cracking that door open had let out an invisible vapor monster. It swirled around her face and wound into her mouth, so thick it could almost be felt on her tongue.

Katie's hands were full, or she'd cover her nose. She was carrying two plastic milk-jugs, one under each arm. One filled with rice-water for Sammi, and one with clean, filtered water for Sarah. A gallon each. She didn't know how many more days they'd be able to keep that up, but with a baby, Sarah would always be the first to get any that was available.

In her hands, she held a covered bowl of stew, thick with beef, carrots, and other vegetables, from their now-dwindling pantry of food they'd managed to pressure-can out of their freezer when the grid went down. Not just *their* freezer, but many people's in the neighborhood.

The group had spent days—and much of their propane—cooking and canning all the defrosting meat on the grill, adding any fresh vegetables that they still had on hand.

Much of that cooking marathon was donated to the group, kept by Katie and Tucker in the garage. It had seemed like *so much* at the time. Too much. People were giving it away willy-nilly, being good neighbors. Katie wondered if they'd known then, that the power would still be out now, would they still have been so generous?

Probably not.

Their garage now housed dozens of jars of stew, soup and vegetables of all variety, depending on who cooked it. But soon, it would all be gone. Feeding a crowd of this size, even if only once a day, was a huge undertaking.

Katie nervously wondered what they'd do then.

After one nearly-failed attempt to go into town to look for food, resulting in bloodshed, Tucker had decided the risk wasn't worth it. Stores had been looted, gangs were everywhere, and she agreed they'd wait it out and see if the power came back, rather than risk their lives again.

But if the grid didn't come up soon, they'd have to send out someone to scavenge. They'd all starve if they just sat around waiting.

The smell grew stronger the closer she got to Sarah's door. No doubt about it now, Sarah would *have* to bring Sammi, and come stay with them. No one could live with *this* smell.

Arriving at Sarah's door, Katie put down her load and knocked. She waited several long moments and then decided to walk around back. It wasn't uncommon for neighbors to seek out some privacy in the evenings in their own backyards; many of them fenced in.

She poked her head over the fence, barely able to see. "Sarah? You back there?" she said softly, not wanting to wake the baby if she was sleeping.

The only answer was the sound of the crickets and cicadas.

They must be in the house, sleeping. But Katie knew

where her extra key was; she'd just take the stuff in and leave it on the counter. She returned to the front porch, gathered up the food and water, hurried back, unlatched the gate, and made her way to the back door, finding the key under the birdhouse sitting on the rail.

"Hello?" Katie called through the kitchen, trying to breathe through her mouth. Plates, cups, and bowls overflowed from the sink. The counters were littered with trash. Chairs were pushed out from the table, all askew, as though someone got up in a hurry and ran out.

The smell was overpowering.

Katie pushed a stack of plates over and put the food on the counter, and the water on the floor, and then peeked into the den to find Sarah sitting in her rocking chair, rocking Sammi soundlessly, her back to the kitchen.

"Oh, there you are. Didn't you hear me calling you?" Katie whispered, relieved to see Sarah up. She stepped into the living room, on tiptoes so that she didn't wake Sammi.

Sarah slowly turned her head, seeing Katie standing beside her now. "No, I'm sorry," she muttered. "Hold on, I'll put Sammi down in her bed."

Katie wiped her hands on her shorts, and held them out. "Let me. I'd love to help. I brought you some supper. You go eat and I'll tuck Sammi in." She stepped in front of Sarah and reached for the baby, swaddled in mounds of blankets. She looked like a tiny burrito. Even her face was covered. "Sarah, isn't it a bit hot in here to have the baby covered like this? How can she even breathe?" She forced a quiet laugh.

Sarah ignored her question and stood, putting Sammi against Katie's shoulder. "Start humming or she'll wake when you walk." She stepped away, into the kitchen, leaving Katie relieved that she at least seemed interested in some food.

Katie hummed and swayed as she walked Sammi to her nursery. The baby was light as a feather. The smell was worse the further she went into the hallway... so much worse she almost gagged again. She was having trouble humming, so strong was the urge to retch. She couldn't believe Sarah could stand this.

She turned and whispered loudly over her shoulder. "Sarah, don't you think we should put her down at my house? You two can stay there until we figure out what to do about this sewage smell."

Sarah ignored her again, and crossed into the kitchen, where Katie heard the clink of a spoon against a bowl. *Oh, well, I'll let her eat in peace,* she thought. *I'll get Sammi down and then talk to her.*

She walked into Sammi's room and approached the crib, a beautiful piece painted white with pink ribbons, and covered with a sheer canopy. She easily held the tiny bundle against her shoulder with one hand, while pulling back the one thin blanket with the other.

Katie jumped back in revulsion and almost screamed, catching herself just in time. She didn't want to wake Sammi.

On top of the sheet, under the blankets, were a handful of tiny, white, fat worms, wiggling around desperately. Katie's face screwed up in revulsion. *What the—?*

She hurried back into the kitchen. "Sarah, there's worms in Sammi's bed!"

Sarah looked at her blankly. "There are?"

"Yes! Where did those come from?"

Sarah's reaction time was sluggish. Finally, she shrugged and took another bite of her stew while Katie stood staring at her in astonishment.

Good Lord, the woman is so exhausted she can't formulate a thought. "Okay, I'll lay her down on the couch for now, and I'll strip her bed. Do you have a clean sheet?" Katie swayed in place with the baby in her arms, waiting.

After an unusually long delay, Sarah put her spoon down and went down the hall. Katie moved into the den. Sarah came back with a sheet and a pillow and mechanically made a pallet on the couch for the baby, tucked it into the back cushion and blocked it off with the pillow, and walked past Katie back into the kitchen.

Katie gently lay Sammi down and looked over her shoulder. It was too hot for these blankets. Not seeing Sarah, she pulled at the corner of the fuzzy blanket to unwrap Sammi, expecting to see the sleeping cherubic face, hopefully now healthy with some color in her cheeks—unlike the last time she'd had a good look at her, when she'd been so sick.

Nothing could have been further from that description.

Katie screamed, and jumped back, falling onto the carpet and scooting away from the horrific bundle, backward with her mouth gaping open. Even from across the room, she could see the fat white worms wriggling in and out of Sammi's eyes—or what once was her eyes, but were now two dark holes in the sunken-in skeletal face.

Sammi looked like a ghoul; a Halloween doll meant to scare.

Katie struggled to her feet, bumped into the rocking chair and nearly fell again. She grabbed the door frame and lunged into the kitchen, away from the puddle of what was Sammi, in an awkward move, and found herself face to face with Sarah.

"What?" Sarah calmly asked.

Katie pointed to the den. "Sammi... she's... she's..."

Sarah walked past her. "You uncovered her. Don't do

that. She's cold," she said, sitting on the edge of the couch and rewrapping her baby, making quiet soothing noises.

A chill ran down Katie's spine.

That baby was *dead.*

Tears streamed down Katie's face, watching Sarah comfort her daughter, who was long past comforting. Had she starved to death? Or was she sick with something else and they hadn't known?

They'd certainly never know now.

Thoughts raced through Katie's mind. *Where would they bury her? Would they need to embalm her or was it too late for that? Could Tucker make a casket? Should they 'save' her body and see if the power came on, in case the officials wanted to do an autopsy? Could they be arrested for burying a body*—she caught herself—for burying *Sammi*?

She couldn't think of that sweet baby girl as just a body.

Not yet.

Katie took a deep breath, and heaved it back out again. The smell, now explained, was even worse from opening the tiny bundle. She stepped forward anyway, and put her hand on Sarah's shoulders. "Sarah."

Sarah ignored her, and continued making hushing noises to Sammi.

"Sarah!" Katie said, louder now.

Sarah turned to her with an incredulous look. "*Shh*! You'll wake her, Katie!"

"No, I won't. She's... gone..." Katie said, lowering her voice on the last word, saying it in nearly a whisper. "She's gone, Sarah. Sammi's not with us anymore," she said, more firmly.

Sarah shook her head, confused, and looked back at Sammi. "What are you talking about? She's right here," she whispered loudly, pointing at Sammi. "Do you not *see* her?"

She glared at Katie, and then back to Sammi. She stopped to stare hard at her daughter.

Katie swallowed a lump in her own throat, and then squeezed her friend's shoulder. She reached up to swipe at the river of tears now falling down Sarah's cheeks. "I do. I see her. But she's not *in* there. She's dead, Sarah."

15

THE FARM

GRAYSON STRETCHED AND YAWNED, and then rolled over to pull Olivia in close, but she was gone. "Olivia?" he called out.

There was no answer.

He looked to the window to see the sun peeking through the blinds. It was barely daybreak. He jumped up and froze... his jaw was pulsing with pain from the bad tooth. Slowly, he slid his pants on, to go look for his wife. It was too early for her to be up, and it was too quiet if she was. But first, he slipped into their bathroom and found his painkillers. He was glad they'd kept them for preps even though he usually refused them. Between what she'd saved from her own prescriptions, and what he'd been prescribed and hadn't used, they had a heaping full bottle...other than the ones Olivia had snuck him recently, against his will.

But now, she wouldn't need to sneak. He was *ready* for some relief.

He picked up the bottle. It was too light. He opened it to find it empty.

What the hell?

He wandered through the house, and looked into the spare room to find Gabby and Jake gone, too. One look in Graysie's room showed Puck bandaged up and resting quietly in Graysie's bed. Ozzie lay curled up at the end of the bed near his feet, lifting his head off of Puck's ankle only long enough to see if their visitor was a threat, and seeing his master, drowsily tucked it back down again.

Grayson noted the bottle of antibiotics on the side table. The first time Puck had been shot, they'd used all natural remedies, and he'd healed well without antibiotics. But this time, he wasn't taking a chance. He cringed thinking of how awful the kid's hand had looked.

But he looked peaceful now, and healthy; and not at all in pain.

He was a walking miracle.

Or a warrior.

The kid had half his finger shot off, and unless you saw his bandaged hand, you'd never know it. The boy was tougher than a pine knot, but Grayson still planned to take him to Tullymore to have Neva check the wound tomorrow. It wasn't that he didn't trust Olivia—but hell, she didn't trust herself. She was insisting someone else look at it, consumed with worry that she'd done something wrong.

Grayson moved on down the hall.

No one was on the couch or the floor; all the blankets were folded up in a neat pile.

No one in the kitchen.

He stepped through to the back porch, finding Gabby & Olivia pouring over a book, and Tina and Tarra walking off toward the woods. Upon hearing the screen door slam, they both turned and smiled at Grayson.

Graysie stood on the step laughing at Jenny as she

scratched around her ears and then stopped, causing Jenny to lean in, nuzzling her hand for more.

Jake and Elmer were nowhere to be seen. "Where's Jake and Elmer?" he asked.

Gabby sadly shrugged her shoulders and looked down the gravel driveway. "Jake's disappeared again. I have no idea where he's been sneaking off to lately. He says he just has a lot on his mind and wants to be alone—a lot."

"Have you noticed he doesn't seem like he feels well a lot, too?"

"Yeah, but he denies it."

Grayson rubbed the sleep out of his eyes, and yawned. "What's everybody else doing up? And where are *they* going?" He nodded toward the two women marching off, each carrying a backpack and a rifle slung over their shoulders, a pistol on their side, and in their hands a roll of fencing—swiped from his container.

Olivia squeezed Grayson's arm and kissed his cheek. "Good morning!"

Hmm. She's in a good mood. His hopes soared as his mind took off in a few possibilities for sneaking private time with his wife. His tooth ached, but she could take his mind off of it...

Puck was sleeping. He could tell everyone else to stay outside.

He watched her turn and pick up a steaming cup, smiling over it and delicately sipping.

Oh, coffee.

Or their new version of it.

Dammit. The smile was definitely for the choffee—Elmer's new name for the chicory drink that mimicked coffee.

Olivia sighed in contentment, and spoke in a low, disapproving voice, so that the women couldn't hear her. "Tina and Tarra are going after those hogs again. They said there's signs of them under the treehouse out in the woods. You need to tell them to let the men do the hunting, Grayson. They're gonna get hurt."

"*Pfft.* Those girls are as, or more, qualified to hunt than any of us menfolk."

Olivia harrumphed. "Whatever." She rolled her eyes. "Gabby and I are going foraging for more of those coffee roots, and some other stuff."

Grayson barely suppressed a laugh, as Gabby waved her hands and shook her head with big eyes behind Olivia's back. Elmer had pulled him aside and explained that Olivia had assumed what she'd tasted at his campfire was *coffee roots*, not hearing him when he clearly said it was chicory. He didn't have the heart to tell her differently. He figured a life-long coffee drinker would know coffee came from *beans* —not roots—but maybe she was purposely convincing herself.

Grayson had let it go, fully expecting her sister, Gabby, to school her and remind her of this fact, but apparently Gabby, and everyone else, was letting it ride.

Whatever works.

Grayson nodded and sat down. "What else are you foraging for?"

Olivia perked up even more. "Dandelions for starters. We're going to make Dandelion Tea, and maybe even some Dandelion Wine. But we can use the whole plant. We can use the leaves for tea, and then roast the roots to make a hot coffee-like drink, too, for a little variety. It's less bitter and less acidic than real coffee. Or we can use the leaves for a fresh salad, or even cook them like spinach. Dandelion is *packed* with calcium and vitamins. We can even make dandelion bread, and cookies and jam."

Grayson held his hand up. "Whoa. How about let's just stick to tea and greens right now? One step at a time, please, honey. Dandelions grow nearly year-round here, so we can tackle the harder stuff later."

Olivia pursed her lips, pouting at his lack of enthusiasm.

Grayson would have to talk to Elmer about putting pie-in-the-sky ideas to Olivia. Right now, he needed to keep her, and the rest of them, focused on the more important tasks.

She crossed her arms.

"What else you lookin' for?"

"Prickly Pear Cactus. I know there's some around. I've seen it somewhere. I read it tastes like green beans if you cook it over a fire. And clover. That's edible. Maybe even some cattails—well, the cattail roots and hearts are what I'm after. The roots are starchy, but the hearts taste like cucumbers."

"Olivia, you know we do still have some food, right?" he asked, now realizing this was about her trying to make up for the preps she was responsible for losing. "We actually *have* food to be picked right now, out in the garden. The *garden* that I need *your* help with."

"I know. But we can always use *more*. We can have lots of variety," she insisted.

He couldn't argue with that. If nothing else, they could do some canning in jars with the pressure cooker over the grill. They could try to can the dandelion greens, just like collards, and maybe the prickly pear too. It wouldn't hurt to try, and they had Mason jars and propane.

He nodded at his wife, looking her over. He tilted his head and looked at her side. "Where's your gun? You're not leaving here without a sidearm."

"Gabby has one."

His eyebrows furrowed.

Behind her, Gabby nodded her head, agreeing with Grayson.

"Go get your gun, honey," he said.

Olivia blew out a breath. "Oh, come on, Grayson. I've already had this argument with Gabby. We may not even get off our property. I've walked this land hundreds of times and never needed a gun before. Y'all are being paranoid."

Grayson shook his head. He was going to have to be firm on this.

Olivia wasn't giving up either. "I'm even more nervous now around a gun, after what happened to Puck." She paused, waiting for him to give in.

He didn't budge. "That was a freak thing. No one is using that gun until Elmer is done taking it apart and putting it back together, and checks all our ammo. It was a *hang fire.* No one could have predicted that—well, no one other than Puck, obviously—because hang fires are more rare than hen's teeth. Even so, usually there's not that long of a lull between pulling the trigger and the gun going off. It would probably never happen again, but that gun's been rotated out until we know more. But you need to get used to carrying your new Baby Desert Eagle anyway."

When they'd found Elmer's truck, he'd been relieved to see Trunk and his goons hadn't found his secret hiding place that housed a set of twin Baby Desert Eagles. Elmer insisted Gabby and Olivia have his '*Beagles*,' since they were twins too, and because he was a sentimental old fool with a soft heart for the women.

Grayson couldn't help but be a bit jealous.

Olivia sighed. "Gabby has one of them. But I'm going to

be squatting a lot. I tried it, and it's uncomfortable on my hip. I feel like I'm gonna drop it."

He crossed his arms. "You're not going to drop it." He matched Olivia's sigh. "Look, I know that gun going off like that scared you. In all my life, I've never seen that happen before. There's like a one in a bazillion chance of it ever happening again. Just keep your gun in your holster and tighten up your belt. Find a place on your hips where it feels natural."

Accepting defeat, but not gracefully, she brushed past her husband. "It'll *never* feel natural, Grayson. And I don't ever *want* it to." The screen door slammed behind her.

Grayson flinched and Gabby shrugged at her brother-in-law. "Sorry. I tried to tell her. She wouldn't listen to me —yet."

"From now on, Gabby, I don't care if you have to throw her down and hog-tie her. She doesn't leave this place without a gun. Nobody does."

Gabby raised her eyebrows at his reprimand. "I know you're aggravated, Grayson, but I didn't have any intention of letting Olivia leave without a gun. We haven't left yet. But you know as well as I do that Olivia has a one-track mind, and at that moment, it was focused on plants. Once she'd put her book away and was ready to go, I was going to remind her again of the gun rule. I know how to manage my own twin sister, brutha, and I've been doing it a lot longer that you have." She winked at him. "We just hadn't made it that far yet."

Grayson hung his head. "Noted. Sorry. I know you handle her better than I do."

She gave him a half-smile and a nod, letting him know everything was fine between them.

"Please keep a close eye on her. I know Puck's accident

really spooked her." He turned and followed his wife into the house. He was going to help her adjust her gun belt, and hopefully smooth things over with her before starting his own day.

Wasn't no one happy when mama wasn't happy.

16

THE FARM

GABBY POKED A LONG ROASTING fork into the flat cactus pad with one hand, and snipped it off with the other, using her Ka-bar knife, careful not to touch the sharp spine needles. She dropped it into the heavy canvas bag they'd brought and stood up, stretching, reminding herself that once they scraped off the needles, they needed to scorch them over a fire to get any pointy stragglers out; no one wanted a mouth full of these pokey things.

Along with the cactus pads, there was also the fruit of the prickly pear cactus, and the book said the fruit was filled with seeds that taste like a combination of kiwi and watermelon. The flowers could be used to make wine; but they weren't gathering those today.

"Okay, I've got a Prickly Pear Cactus pad for each person at the table. We'll stop at that for now. We don't want to take them all when we don't really need them... yet," she rambled, expecting her sister to argue. These might come in real handy if ever they lost water, too. Not only were they good for eating, but they were filled with water and a juicy pulp.

No response from Olivia.

She looked around. "Olivia? Where are you?"

No answer.

Olivia had wandered off, *yet again*, with her nose in that Wild Foraging book, looking for other things to identify and harvest. Their bags were full now. They'd found plenty of the 'coffee root' that Elmer had described, actually drawing them a picture, *and* sending one from his pile with them—whispering to Gabby *not* to call it Chicory Root or Choffee when talking to Olivia—and they had six bags of dandelions with roots tied to their backpacks.

Olivia had decided she wanted to sauté the dandelion greens. One bag would cook down to nearly nothing, so they'd gathered plenty for one full meal, or maybe enough to can two jars, depending on how much time they had before they wilted away. They'd agreed to work the garden when they returned, before experimenting with their new foods, and after Olivia changed Puck's bandage.

She was surprised at what a trooper Olivia had been in dealing with such a gruesome accident. She'd done a great job with Puck—again. Olivia always did have a quiet, inner strength. Growing up, it was her that had taken lead on their little girl group of three, with herself and Emma.

But when she'd married badly, she hadn't breathed a word to Gabby for the longest time about the beatings she had endured in first marriage; instead, she'd stoically suffered in silence.

She hoped Olivia had at least won *some* points with Tina and Tarra for her bravery—if Elmer could prove she hadn't touched the trigger, sending off the bullet that shot off Puck's finger. It'd all happened so quick, and no one other than Puck and Olivia could say for sure if the trigger *had* been pulled. But both said *neither* had touched the gun.

Gabby believed them. Olivia may have held back the truth long ago, but that was to protect her sisters. Olivia would never lie to protect herself.

If Tina and Tarra had seen Olivia before she'd found Grayson, they'd have seen her for what she really was, deep down. Gabby was glad to see the layers peeling away a bit at a time to reveal that within her sister again; they were all going to need to toughen up in this new world.

Gabby stepped out away from the cactus and turned in a circle, wondering which way to go looking for her wayward sister now. She was hot, tired, and frustrated. For hours now she'd had to chase Olivia as she continuously disappeared behind every stand of trees and pile of brush while she complained about the gun; the weight of it, the wobbling of it, the *smell* of it... as if she could actually *smell* the gun oil.

Could she?

She took a few steps and startled to a stop when she heard a loud scream.

Rushing forward in that direction, she broke through a stand of brush, thorns and thistles scratching at her face and arms, and pulled her sidearm from her holster.

"*Shhh*," Olivia whispered, catching Gabby's arm on the other side of the brush and stopping her.

"Did you scream?" Gabby loudly whispered back.

"*Shhh!*" Olivia repeated, her finger to her lips. "No. Not me. Look." She pointed.

Gabby followed her finger.

Sitting at a dilapidated wooden picnic table were two very small, and very *dirty* children; a boy and a girl with light blonde hair and dirty clothes. They were skinny, and pale as ghosts as they huddled over paper, quietly scribbling with their heads down, in the shade of a huge oak tree. The boy was half a head taller than his little sister, who couldn't have been more than six years old, if that.

"Who lives here?" Gabby whispered.

Olivia looked around. "I've never seen this place. We must've walked much further off the property than I thought."

Behind the children was an old mobile home, the tin roof crumpled and rusted with age, windows broken out with curtains hanging limp in the humid, still air. A set of worn steps leaned to the right and the metal door hung open, like a dark gaping mouth missing a big front tooth.

"Who screamed?" Gabby whispered, lowering her gun.

Olivia shrugged her shoulders. "I don't know, but it wasn't them."

Another scream rang out, sending a shiver down Gabby's spine, but the children didn't even flinch.

She spun her finger in the air in a circle, telling Olivia they needed to check out the back of the yard, and she crept along the edge of the woods, her sister following closely behind her, both trying not to get the attention of the little boy and girl.

On the other side of the trailer an old truck was parked, one door hanging open. A man stood in the open door, his pants down around his knees, bent over two more smaller, skinny white legs that were barely visible between his own, covered in crazy long knee-socks of rainbow colors shoved into sandals.

Gabby couldn't see the owner of the smaller set, but could see from the position of their legs that she was laying bent over the seat, on her stomach.

Bumping uglies.

Another man leaned against the truck, looking the other way, smoking a joint, and oblivious to the world around him. With his greasy long hair and stained wife-beater shirt, he looked like a strung-out, botched-up bodyguard. He had a gun strapped to his side. At his feet lay an open bag. Gabby could see a tall bottle of cheap liquor, a roll of toilet paper, and a pack of cookies sticking out the top.

The man over the woman kept moving, and not gently. The woman didn't make a sound.

"Do you think that's consensual?" Olivia whispered.

Gabby turned to her sister and gave her 'the look.' "I don't know. She's not fighting, but we both know that doesn't mean she wants it. There's two of them and only one of her. But she's not screaming either, so maybe that was someone else from inside the trailer. Let's go talk to the kids. See if they know these guys, or if someone else is here. There could be more men—or women—inside."

She backed up, pulling Olivia with her, as a determined look came over her. They'd all seen their share of this sort of thing up close and personal. Gabby hoped that it wasn't what they thought it was. If it was, or even if it wasn't, it would probably bring them both nightmares tonight. They were no strangers to night terrors; they haunted their family's dreams.

They crept back to the front yard where they could see the kids and the door. Gabby whispered to Olivia. "You stay here and cover me."

"Cover you?" Olivia whispered loudly, around a look of disbelief. "What are you talking about, Gabby? I don't know how to *cover* someone!"

Gabby slowly pulled Olivia's pistol out of her holster and placed it in her hand. "Don't play dumb. You *know* how to shoot this. Just keep it pointed toward me—not *at* me—and if one of those men comes around and tries to shoot me, you shoot him first."

Olivia rolled her eyes. "Geez, Gabby. This isn't a movie. No one is gonna shoot at you. Just find out if the woman in the truck is the one that screamed. That'll tell us all we need to know. *Hurry!* They might be hurting her."

Gabby smoothed down her mussed hair so she didn't look like a wild, crazy woman, and ran to the kids, stopping short and coming to a walk before moving into their line of vision. She didn't want to startle them. She whistled a song, the first one she could think of... the tune to Sponge Bob Square Pants. The kids turned around with wide eyes, and watched her approach, their crayons held in mid-air.

The little boy scooted closer to his sister, putting his arm around her and pulling her tight against him, an attempt at bravery when Gabby could clearly see he was as afraid as she was.

Gabby squatted down between them. "Hi. My name is Gabby. What's your name?"

The boy slowly answered. "Brody." He stuck his chin out in false bravado, and then looked down at his sister. Her lip poked out and quivered. He took her hand and held it tight. "This is my sister, Briar."

Gabby gently ran her hand over the child's dirty, tangled hair. "It's okay, sweetie. I won't hurt you. I have a sister, too," she said brightly. "She's right over there, and she looks just like me. We're twins." Gabby pointed behind her to the woods. "We heard a scream. Is everyone okay here?"

Brody looked over his shoulder, toward the trailer. "That was my mama. She always screams like that when those men come over. She told us to stay here."

"Does your mom wear rainbow knee-socks?" Gabby asked him.

Brody nodded slowly.

So, she was the screamer.

"Is anyone else here? Someone inside the house?" Gabby asked.

The boy shook his head no, with wide eyes.

Gabby looked toward the woods and found Olivia, nodded, confirming from Olivia's face she could hear the kids' answers, and then turned back to the kids. She looked at the papers on the picnic table. The little girl's picture showed two little stick figure people standing on either side of a bigger stick figure; a larger one, clearly a man, wearing a ball cap. In his hand was a ball with three holes in it. *The daddy? Bowling?*

Where was the mama in the picture?

The little stick figures beside him were drawn with big smiles—smiles that were nowhere to be seen on these children in real life.

The little boy's paper showed a remarkably well-drawn picture of a hotdog and a pizza. "Are you hungry?" Gabby asked them.

Both the kids vigorously nodded.

"Go over to my sister. She's really nice. She'll give you a snack out of her bag. I'll be there in a minute." She stood up. "Go ahead," she encouraged them with a smile. "She's got fruit snacks."

The kids stood to obey her immediately, and Brody kept a hold of his little sister's hand. He turned to where Gabby pointed and said, "Where?"

Gabby turned to look behind her.

Olivia was gone.

17

THE FARM

OLIVIA EASED up the side of the yard to get closer to the truck, bent slightly over and awkwardly gripping her gun with two hands. She took a deep breath, trying to control her trembling. Whether she was shaking from holding the gun awkwardly, or shaking from anger, she didn't know.

Images of her sisters, Gabby and Emma, flashed through her mind. They too had been in this position at one time, a long time ago; at the mercy of a stronger human being. Someone taking advantage of the weaker sex and forcing themselves onto them in sick ways. She was the older sister —only by three minutes from Gabby—but she'd always taken that role seriously.

She'd failed to protect her sisters back then; she'd had no idea it was going on. Struggling to find a way free from her own monster, she'd missed all *their* signs. She'd let them down. She thought about her own first marriage, and the abuse she'd escaped; hers was fists and feet... and she wondered which was worse, and not for the first time. To be taken against your will, or beaten? Was the devil you knew better than the devil you didn't?

It didn't matter.

Both types of abusers were the devil. Men who used their dominance to overpower women in *any* way were the scourge of the earth. They were a blight on humanity. A menace to society, and in *this* new society it would only get worse. She couldn't allow it to go unpunished.

Not anymore.

The woman in the truck screamed again, and again, and again, and Olivia raised her gun.

"Get off of her!" she yelled. "Now."

The scroungy man leaning against the truck snapped his head up, and gave a little scream of his own, dropping his smoke and raising both hands, palms out.

"*Umm.* Gary?" he yelled to his friend, keeping his face and eyes pointed at Olivia.

Gary, the name of the man mounting the woman now revealed, ignored him, and the woman began to scream continuously, barely taking a breath.

Olivia cringed at her cries, and raised the gun higher, pointing it directly at the man from twenty-five feet away. "Tell him to get *off* of that woman right now," she said in a strangely calm, but loud and scary voice, that didn't sound as though it belonged to her. She hadn't even thought to speak... the words were coming out on their own.

"Gary! Get your *ass* out here! Hurry!" Scroungy Guard yelled desperately, a bead of sweat running down his temple. His legs shook and his hands vibrated in fear of the wild-eyed woman standing over him. He lifted one knee, and then dropped it quick, kicking the truck behind him with his boot heel.

Gary, obviously otherwise engaged to the point of deafness, didn't heed the call.

The woman continued to scream, and Olivia squeezed

her eyes shut and pulled the trigger, landing her first bullet in the passenger side-view mirror of the truck, shattering the glass. The gun kicked up, nearly hitting her in the nose.

Limp-wristed it, she heard Tina's voice in her head say.

Scroungy Guard dropped to the ground. "Holy shit! *Gary!*"

Gary's legs stilled and his head finally popped up. He looked out the front window, caught sight of Olivia and ducked again, skedaddling all the way *into* the truck with his britches still down, crawling over the top of the poor woman laying on her stomach, half in and half out of the vehicle. She climbed in behind him, moving quickly in her panic, too, and disappeared into the floor.

"What the hell's going on out there?" Gary yelled, keeping his head down.

The air filled with the smell of gunpowder and the sound of silence; even the birds were afraid to make a peep with Olivia holding a shaking, smoking gun. She stood still, pointing the gun at the front of the truck.

"Um... there's some lady out here. She said to get off of Glenda," Scroungy Guard yelled.

"What the hell for?" Gary asked in disbelief. "Who is it?"

"Who the hell knows? Just *do it*!" Scroungy guard answered, keeping his eyes on a silent Olivia, while trying to press himself as far into the ground and against the truck as he could.

A long moment passed, and then Gary and 'Glenda' slithered out of the truck, pulling up their pants with one hand, while holding the other up in the air.

"Move away from the truck," Olivia snapped, her voice brisk.

The couple moved a few feet away from the truck, giving Olivia a perfect shot.

"Come over here," Olivia said to the woman, waving her gun beside her.

The woman bit her lip and looked from Olivia to Gary, and then back to Olivia. Her face scrunched up. "Why?"

Olivia blinked twice, rapidly. "To get *away* from them," she hissed, not believing the woman's stupidity. Maybe she was disorientated?

"But... *why*?" the woman asked again.

Olivia paused in her answer, looking from Glenda to Gary, and then to the man on the ground and back to Glenda. She was getting a very bad vibe from this woman now. "Isn't he raping you?"

"Hell no, I'm not raping her!" Gary answered for her. "She's working off a trade. This is business."

Olivia startled at his words. *Could that be true? She wanted it? What kind of woman—* "Is he... telling the truth?" she asked Glenda in a shaky voice, now having problems keeping the gun up; her arms were so tired. She took a deep breath and waited for Glenda's answer.

Glenda didn't have the grace to look down when she answered. Defiantly, she said, "Yeah, I guess," and then added, hesitantly, "I mean, I need what he's bringing for it."

Olivia swallowed hard, and then felt a hand on her shoulder. She whipped her head around, nearly dropping her gun.

Gabby stepped up beside her sister and pointed her own gun, more to protect her and Olivia than to threaten with.

Olivia turned back to Glenda, taking the opportunity to lower her own pistol and rest her arms, since Gabby now had them covered. "Then why were you screaming?"

Glenda shrugged. "He pays more for screaming. A girl has needs, yanno?" Her face twitched, making the many scabs dance, and she furtively tried to scratch at her head with the backside of her thumb while her hands were still splayed open, in the air.

Junkie.

It was obvious now.

"Your *kids* have needs too. They look like they're starving. Why are they bringing you liquor and toilet paper instead of more food? The only thing I see here is a pack of cookies," Gabby said, her eyes falling onto the sores on the woman's arms and face, and her thin, stringy hair.

Olivia raised her gun again, pointing at Gary, fire in her eyes.

Gary and Scroungy Guard both spoke at once, their hands in the air. "Wait!"

"We'd give her food instead if that's what she *wanted.* She don't want that. We went out and found exactly what she asked for," said Gary, in defense.

"And some of what she got isn't in the bag. Plus, she needs her juice," Scroungy Guard added. "That was extra."

"Yeah. This bitch don't care about those kids," Scroungy Guard spit out. "She's *giving* it away to anyone that brings her a bottle of liquor or a fix."

Olivia's finger squeezed the trigger, and the gun went off, splitting the air with the deafening shot. The dirt danced in front of the man.

"Olivia!" Gabby yelled. "What the hell are you doing? You could 'a killed him!"

Olivia dropped her gun onto the ground and stared at it, then looked at the man crab walking toward the back of the truck, his eyes wide with fear. "Stop right there." He froze again. "You're still taking advantage of her. *Making* her have sex to feed her kids." She bent down and grabbed her gun again.

"We didn't make her do shit. She offered. Hell, she

offered the *kids* to us, too! I'm telling ya, she don't give a shit about them," Gary yelled in defense. "I brought the cookies on my own for the children. She didn't even *ask* for food. They're up for trade, too. Just ask her yourself."

Gabby and Olivia both gasped.

Surely, he didn't mean—?

Did he?

The woman didn't even try to deny it. Olivia narrowed her eyes and stomped forward, her gun straight and steady, and pointed it at the woman's head. "We're taking those kids with us," she growled at her.

The woman held her hands up even higher, not arguing. She nodded repeatedly, looking all the world like a strung-out bobblehead doll.

Gary side-stepped slowly away from Glenda, lowering his hands, now that he wasn't the target of Olivia's anger anymore. He shoved his hands in his pockets and looked around, licking his lips. "Look, if y'all want the boy, I'll be happy to take the girl off her hands. I'll keep her fed." He squinted his eyes at Glenda. "I hadn't got around to *my* offer yet. I've got another four bottles in the truck. Trade ya fair and square... the little girl for the hooch—and by hooch, I don't mean yours."

Suddenly, he became the target again.

18

TULLYMORE

TUCKER PUSHED the wheelbarrow through the quiet neighborhood, heading back toward his house with a large load of dandelions and dandelion roots that he and the kids had picked from a neighboring field. He hadn't seen a soul outside as they'd re-entered from a short cut through a grown-over back yard. The kids had been released from duty and ran ahead, hoping to get some time to nap before dinner. The entire 'hood was taking a siesta to beat back the heat, with the exception of the security team who was posted at the entrance.

The kids weren't being punished. They'd sworn they'd not been back in the pool, and that none of them had touched a hose. But the food was running out and it *had* to be replenished. With the stores being cleaned out within days of the grid going down, they had no other choice but to forage and hunt once their supplies ran low. Tucker firmly believed in keeping everyone busy, even the teenagers, from dawn 'til dusk trying to gather more food; and only allowed a break during the hottest hours of the day.

Besides, they'd been warned worse was coming. He wanted to be prepared this time, as well as he could be.

Tucker enjoyed working outside though. He'd always had a blue-collar job before and relished the freedom from a corporate life and a desk he'd always been sure he'd feel chained to. Working with his own two hands outside made him feel alive, even before it was a necessity.

If food was plenty, he'd take this new lifestyle over the old one. Not much had changed for him, other than he didn't leave his own neighborhood to work, and now he had an opportunity to spend more time with the kids; even if they complained every minute of it.

He stopped abruptly at voices coming from Curt's house, turning his head to see a strange motorcycle in the driveway. The motorcycle was laden with full saddlebags, the flaps pushed up with boxes and cans of food haphazardly jammed in.

Curt followed an ink-covered man in camo fatigues out the side-door of his garage, and they headed for the motorcycle, both working fast to stuff more food in amongst the already overflowing bags.

Tucker set the wheelbarrow down and hurried over, surprising them both. "Whoa! What's going on here? Where'd you get all this food?"

Curt and the stranger exchanged panicked looks and both pointed at each other. Curt gave a weak laugh, and shook his head. "No... he means..." he trailed off, not finishing his thought, and instead changed the subject. "Tucker, have you met my cousin? This is Nat. He's National Guard."

Surprised at how cordial Curt was being to him, and assuming it could only be due to good news, Tucker wiped his hands on his pants and shook the young man's hand. "Really? So, what's happening?"

Nat's eyes widened and he looked to Curt as though for permission to answer. Curt shrugged, and flipped over one hand in the air. Nat stuffed his hands in his pockets. "I came to warn Curt—warn all of y'all. Something big is going down."

Tucker's smile melted off his face. He scoffed politely. "We sorta heard that already, but what? Is it bigger than the grid going down? They getting it back up soon? We haven't heard anything, from anyone—FEMA wouldn't tell us shit. Did the National Guard send you out here?"

Nat shook his head. "FEMA? They've been here?" He looked around guiltily. "No. I'm on my own. Personal courtesy; Curt is family. The grid's not coming back up anytime soon, and rumor is that worse *is* coming. Y'all need to move on out, or they're gonna move you out."

"Move out to where? That summer camp FEMA told us about? Where do we go? And who are *'they'*...FEMA?"

Nat licked his lips. "Look. I don't know anything 'cept I overheard a conversation. Get somewhere safe, quick. Curt can fill you in. I gotta go." Quickly, he gave Curt a one-armed hug, threw his leg over the motorcycle, and started it up. "Good luck, man," he said to his cousin as he tore out of the driveway.

"Wait," Tucker said, holding up a hand. "Come talk to everyone. Talk to all of us."

Nat ignored him, not looking back as he streaked out of the neighborhood.

"Wait! What are we running from?" Tucker yelled over the scream of the motorcycle, now almost deafening in their newly-quieted world without power. The sound reverberated through the entire neighborhood as the motorcycle tore toward the entrance, disappearing around a corner, bringing people out of their houses.

Tucker looked at Curt. "What was that all about?"

"Man, I don't know." Curt turned to walk away with a shrug. "Nat always has been a bit off. I'll see you later."

"Wait. Where'd that food come from?"

Curt kept walking, giving Tucker his back. "It was his."

"I saw you carrying it *out* of your garage." Tucker hurried past Curt toward the open garage, and Curt tried to stop him, getting shoved back easily, as Tucker beat him to the door. "What the hell, man?" he said as he stood looking at Curt's Nissan Pathfinder that was parked inside, all the doors wide open.

Food was stacked up from the seats to the ceiling and filled the cargo space completely up. "Thought your side was running low too? Looks like you have enough here to feed a small army. Why is it in the truck?"

"It's not mine," Curt said loudly, getting in front of Tucker and pushing him back, then shutting the doors behind him, but not before Tucker saw a case marked *baby formula*. Curt stood looking up at Tucker, a nervous sheen forming on his face. "This isn't my people's food..." He paused. "Well, it is, but not—"

Tucker balled up his fists. "—Thought you said it was his? And if you have all that, why are they asking our side for food and saying they're hungry all the time? Why is it in the car?"

"Listen, man. We're all in trouble here. Let's not add fuel to the fire. I'm feeding everybody the best I can. You see anyone starving to death? Don't believe everything you hear."

Fire boiled in Tucker's veins. "Yeah, actually. I *have* seen someone starve to death, now that you mention it."

Curt's face flamed and he began to back pedal. "The baby formula was just given to me on trade. I was going to take it over right now for that baby."

"Too late for that," Tucker hissed through clenched teeth.

"No, it's not. It's not even dinner time. I'll take it right now."

"I said, too *late* for that. *Sammi* died. That was her name. *Sammi*. And he didn't bring it on that motorcycle. There's no way that box would've fit into one of those saddlebags. You're a damn liar, Curt. And a murderer."

Curt held his hands up, palms out. "Now hold on just a minute. That baby has been sick since they brought it home. Everybody knows that woman's milk dried up too soon. It probably wouldn't have lasted much longer even with the formula."

Tucker's eyes bulged. "It?"

"She!"

A vein ticked in Tucker's neck.

Curt bit his lip. "Listen. How about you take what you want. You got kids, right? Take whatever you need. But not too much, I have to keep feeding my half of the neighborhood with the rest of it."

"You're trying to buy my silence?"

Curt waited silently with a look of apprehension.

Tucker slowly shook his head, staring daggers at Curt. "Not a chance," he said, and walked back to his wheelbarrow, nearly shaking the ground with the weight of his steps. "I'll be back."

19

TULLYMORE

JAKE SWIPED his forearm across his face, wiping at the sweat. His head pounded in rhythm with his pounding heart. He felt terrible—as usual.

They'd left Puck and Graysie standing in line at Neva's house as he and Grayson looked for Tucker. They'd been pointed to the direction of the new graveyard, after hearing the devastating news about Sammi.

Jake could hardly believe it. He hadn't known Sarah and her husband well—not as well as Gabby had—but they were his neighbors. He was sorry that they hadn't been able to bring back what Sarah had needed on their one trip to town that had led to bloodshed when the grid first went down. But he'd truly thought Sammi was going to make it after Neva had given them the tip on the rice water.

He felt bad that he'd missed the funeral, but didn't regret Gabby missing it... this news would tear her up. She and Sarah had been good friends, and she'd held that baby many times.

They'd brought Puck so that Neva could check out his finger—or lack of a finger. In addition, Grayson's toothache had become too much to bear, so they'd risked another trip to Jake's old neighborhood to see if Neva could provide him too with a different treatment, something more serious than what she'd given him before, but something short of pulling it, which he'd made his mind up wasn't happening without a real dentist involved.

Neva had a line of people ahead of them, and not wanting to waste time, they'd left the kids there for her to take a look at Puck first.

Graysie was going to try to hold a place in line for Grayson too, while they sought out Tucker to talk about Trunk and the gang arriving at the farm and nearly killing them all. They didn't need to ask who'd sent him. They'd already heard the suspicions when first arriving at Tullymore. Seems the people in his group weren't that loyal to him by now.

Grayson wanted to talk to Tucker about what to do about Curt.

Curt knew too much, and he obviously *talked* too much, too.

Jake also had something to talk to Neva about and hoped he'd get a chance, before they left. He had his own demons to bear and they were getting the best of him. He needed help—from someone. And that someone *couldn't* be his family.

He wiped the beads of sweat from his forehead again, and could almost feel it re-forming two seconds later as he and Grayson crossed the farthest yard in the neighborhood, and entered the woods where they'd been told Tucker and a few of the guys had gone to check on Sammi's grave in the spot they'd chosen for a make-shift graveyard. They pushed through the brush and stepped out into the clearing, and then stopped in surprise, looking from Tucker to the boys, then to Kenny and Xander, and finally at Curt who sat crumpled at the base of a tree. "Whoa! What's going on here?" Jake asked.

"He did it!" Curt yelled in a garbled voice, pointing at Tucker. "Help me."

Curt was on the ground, leaned against a tree with his jaw hanging askew, like a beat-up door with missing hinges. The side of his face had been kicked in, reminding Jake of the long-faced mask from the movie, *Scream*. His skin was ashen and his eyes unfocused, as though he'd just awoken, and a bright river of red streamed from his nose.

While the men watched in disgust, Curt awkwardly and painfully spit into one hand, delivering shards of his teeth. He quickly threw them onto the ground in horror.

Even Grayson cringed. "Damn. He's broke up worse than a fat kid's Big Wheel."

Tucker had the grace to look abashed, albeit furious. Kenny was fidgeting nervously, but Xander stood defiant, arms crossed. He gave a firm nod when Jake's eyes fell once again upon him. Tucker's two boys, Zach and Isaac, dropped their heads and stared at the ground, unsure of how to react. Their father had schooled them all their lives on using martial arts for violence.

Jake hoped this was justified... or Tucker might just lose the respect of his own kids.

Grayson stepped over and squatted down in front of Curt, staring at his deformed and bloody face for a long moment. He scratched his short beard, studying the broken man. "Why the long face, bud?"

Jake rolled his eyes at Grayson's insensitive—yet funny —remark, and Curt mumbled something incoherent in answer, his hands moving aimlessly through the air, as though he wanted to touch his face, but wouldn't dare. The pain he was in was clearly excruciating.

"How'd this happen?" Jake asked.

"Roundhouse kick," Tucker muttered.

Jake looked at Tucker's feet, clad in steel-toed work boots. He cringed, his mouth pinching his jaw. One look at Curt and he'd known it'd been by Tucker's hand—or foot in this case. He sighed, impatient. "I meant, *why*? What's going on?"

"That piece of shit was holding out on us. He had baby formula the whole time. Sarah's baby *died*. She might've lived if he'd given it to us," Tucker spit out in fury, glaring at Curt.

Grayson's eyebrows raised. "This true?" he asked Curt.

Curt began a red-bubble-filled rampage, his hands slicing the air in fury, punctuating his unintelligible explanation. His finger pointed at Kenny accusingly.

Kenny and the boys all nodded, and Kenny spoke up, although weakly, as though he didn't want a part of this. "It's true. I saw a truck full of food with my own eyes. He had a case of baby formula in there, and a whole lot of other food. Enough to make a big difference around here. He was hoarding it for himself," he finished, and kicked at the dirt, his eyes pointed down.

Curt screamed in anguish and spit a slew of unintelligible words at Kenny, still pointing at him, punctuating the air with each garbled word.

They ignored him.

Kenny cleared his throat. "Um. He's also the one who told that gang where you lived, Grayson. Sent them out to your farm when they were looking for your wife and Gabby."

Curt attempted to stand, yelling through a mess of blood

and seemingly trying to hold his jaw up with one hand, the other pushing up off the ground.

Grayson kicked his hand out from under him, knocking him back to the ground, and eyeballed Tucker. "Figured it was him. Where's all the food now?"

Tucker was furious. "He had it all packed up in a truck, and his wife took off with it when Kenny went to talk to them—guess they were hoarding gas too. She left this deadbeat standing there alone, probably to atone for what he did. Kenny said she didn't even wave goodbye to him. You gonna try to stop this?"

It was no secret Grayson and Tucker didn't see eye to eye on much and squabbled nearly every time they were together. Tucker was expecting a fight from him.

"No. I stand with you." Grayson spit on the ground in front of Curt. "This makes him a murderer in these times, and a no-good rat, too. May as well kick leaves over him now anyway. There's no medical care—not that can fix that jaw. He'd be nothing but trouble from here on out," Grayson said, and shrugged, and then looked to Jake for his thoughts.

Jake exchanged a stupefied look with Grayson, who didn't blink an eye.

He turned to Tucker, who stood with pursed lips.

Surely, they didn't mean it. Maybe Curt was responsible for that baby's death, but that didn't make him a *murderer*. Kicking leaves over someone would make *them* the murderers. Jake shook his head. "No, Grayson. We ain't *killing* somebody."

Tucker ran a hand down his face, ending at the now apocalyptic-beard that covered his skin. "Look, Jake. No offense, but you tucked tail and ran from Tullymore. You don't get to make the decisions if you aren't living here. You left all that on *me*. You wanna step in and be the boss, be my guest. I'll gladly hand it over. But not if you're gonna hop back into Ruby and haul ass again."

Jake could understand his frustration. And he was hearing what Tucker wasn't saying, too. He and Tucker were friends. He was sure Tucker and Katie were wondering why they hadn't been invited out to the farm. But it wasn't Jake's place to bring more people. It was Grayson's farm and the majority of the preps that they had left were his, too. "I'm sorry, Tucker. That's where Gabby's family is—*my* family. I had to go, and maybe I have no say-so, but I'm gonna say it anyway. Don't you guys think killing someone is taking this a bit far?" He looked around the group at all the hardened faces. Even the kids seemed to silently disagree with him.

Only Kenny seemed unsure, and he wasn't speaking up —or even looking up.

Grayson's ire raised. "That man nearly killed us too, Jake. You heard what Kenny's wife told us. Penny said *Curt* sent Trunk and his goons to the farm. If it hadn't been for Puck, *your* wife would be dead; *and* my daughter. Maybe all of us."

Jake absorbed that, his heart clenching again at the thought of losing Gabby, and his eyes going back to Curt's face, which now showed more panic than pain. Curt shook out a no, emphatically twisting his broken face left to right. The panic on his face told the tale, though. He *was* the rat. And once a rat, always a rat.

They shouldn't show mercy to this guy. He realized that now.

Jake would prefer a judge and a jury handle it. And maybe they'd need to set something like that up later, if the world didn't get set back to right. But, in this situation, they'd have to pass sentence themselves. If Curt threw them under the bus to one more bad guy, sending people to the farm, the consequences could be deadly.

He looked up and met Grayson's eyes.

Grayson nodded, seeing agreement in them. "Let's get this rat killin' underway," he said.

"*Nooooo*," Curt warbled pathetically, followed by a rant of unidentified pleading, of which they didn't understand a word, other than one that sounded like "*Kenny*!"

Jake glanced at Kenny to see if he would bend at the man's pleas for help. Kenny stared at the ground, ignoring him.

Jake jerked his head toward the path "Let's go." He couldn't let the kids see this. "Everybody but Grayson and Tucker is with me."

The boys looked at their dad, morbid curiosity painting their faces. Tucker nodded. "Go with Jake, and don't breathe a word of this to anyone; especially the women."

Jake led the way, with Tucker's two boys lagging behind him, and Xander and Kenny bringing up the rear. Xander hurried them along with gentle prods, until they all stepped out of the woods, and kept walking.

Kenny brought up the rear, walking slower than anyone. Stopping a few times, hesitating, and then continuing as though he himself walked the Green Mile.

Tucker and Grayson stood over Curt, as he sniveled and begged for mercy with a tsunami of tears, blood and whimpers.

Tucker looked to Grayson standing silent, his arms folded across his chest, as though trying to keep himself under control. He could see him vibrating with anger as he stood over Curt.

He looked down at Curt and thought about that innocent baby.

Sammi.

And her grieving mother, Sarah, who was lost to them too. They'd had to pry the dead baby out of her arms as she refused to believe there was no life left in her. Sarah hadn't come out of her house since then, barely eating and staring at the bedroom ceiling for hours upon hours. She'd told Katie she wanted to die with Sammi; to be buried with Sammi in her arms to protect her from the *worms* that she'd finally seen and tried to pick out of her daughter's face, one by one, as though it were nothing more than plucking grass from her hair after a playful romp in the yard.

That woman was totally alone now, at least until her husband found his way home from where ever he was stationed when the grid went down. Curt had taken away his happy homecoming, too, if he ever made it home—instead, he'd be met with his baby in a grave and his wife out of her mind with grief.

He took a deep breath; he wouldn't feel bad about this.

He hoped.

Tucker's hand hovered over the gun that he now wore on his side. He almost agreed with Jake. This was crazy...crazier than anything he'd ever imagined he'd be involved in. Everything felt surreal. Were they actually going to end someone's life? *On purpose?* He himself had said this was now the Wild West, and finally, he truly believed his own words.

He dropped his hand away from the gun.

He couldn't do it.

Not that way.

He knew there'd come a time—sooner rather than later—that he'd be forced to live or die by a gun, but that day wasn't today. There were other ways to shut up a rat, and they were less noisy, too.

"I'll take care of it," Tucker said and stepped closer to Curt. Although he didn't want to touch the bloody mess that was now Curt, with his training, he knew more than one way to kill a man without wasting a bullet.

Curt threw himself backward, quickly crab-walking away from Tucker in cowardly fashion as Tucker moved to chase him down, walking slowly toward him. He hoped he fought. It'd be easier if Curt fought him. Easier on his conscience anyway.

Curt pleaded another stream of jagged, muffled words. "*Don't! Jury*! Law!" were the only three they could understand, as he whined through broken, bloody teeth and a hanging jaw. He scooted faster, trying to back-crawl his way to freedom. Tucker followed until Curt's path was blocked by a tree, his back shoved up against the rough bark.

Curt looked around frantically, realizing it was the end of the road.

Grayson calmly answered, "There is no law right now. Things will be going back to the good old days; eye for an eye and tooth for a tooth. Consider yourself judged," he said. "You'll get a second judging at the pearly gates."

Curt sobbed wordlessly and Tucker visibly cringed.

"—Dammit, Curt." Grayson impatiently stepped in front of Tucker. "You *lived* life like a coward. Can't you even *die* like a man?" He half-turned and pushed Tucker back. "Ears!"

Tucker covered his ears.

Grayson pulled his gun from his holster and shot Curt between the eyes.

20

TULLYMORE

SCREAMS RANG OUT, startling Tucker and Grayson even worse than the thud of Curt's dead body hitting the ground.

Both looked around with wide eyes. Had they been seen?

A chorus of barking filled the air. Tucker knew those barks. Those were *his dogs*, and something was very wrong.

"You go," Grayson said. "I'll take care of him."

They both stared at Curt, finally silenced.

"With *what*? Do you see a shovel anywhere?" Tucker answered tersely. "Oh shit, Grayson. You—we—shouldn't have done this. He's dead."

"Shut the hell up, Tucker. Of course he's dead. He just got lead poisoning. Pull yourself together. We all decided this was best. Now go!" Grayson ordered, pointing toward the houses. "Go see what's up. If anyone asks, you left Curt in here talking to me. Gun went off accidentally. Everything's fine."

Tucker ran, realizing he was shivering in the heat. *Shock*, he guessed. He broke through the woods just in time to see a box truck recklessly speeding down the street, with a man hanging out the window, his meaty arms covered in tattoos pointing a gun—

—at his boys, Zach and Isaac, who were standing in the road waving their arms and yelling, and then giving chase on foot, cutting through a yard and running like the wind, lightning fast, as only teenage boys can do, breaking the distance between them too fast.

Pop, pop, pop.

He ran faster, his heart pumping...screaming, "Boys, get out of the road. Get down!" as the truck slid around a corner, the tires squealing. *Please lord*, he prayed. *Please let them miss.*

Pop, Pop.

Zach hearing his father's bellow, answered in return, without breaking his stride. "They got our dogs, Dad!"

"Forget the dogs! They have a gun," Tucker screamed. He pulled his own gun out of the holster, knowing it was too far to make a shot, but not knowing what else to do, just as the shooter in the truck took aim again.

At his boys.

He fell to one knee and brought the gun up, his arms shaking, as thoughts flooded in: *His children laying still with a bleeding hole in the hearts. Katie grieving over their boys shot in the middle of the road. Him shoveling dirt over their still-boyish faces. Karma... coming for him for what they just did to Curt.*

Fuck Karma.

He pulled the trigger, aiming at the truck, again and again and again...until he'd unloaded the full magazine, every shot too short.

At the same time as the shooter split the air with his own lead.

Isaac, the younger of the two, dove for the ground,

sliding on the grass as though stealing third base, coming to a stop and covering his head with his hands.

But Zach ran on, gaining on the truck who had to slow for another corner to make its getaway out of the neighborhood, running straight into the path of a barrage of bullets as though made of steel, with no regard for the fact he was being shot at.

Time froze as the shooter half-crawled out the window to get a better shot. His muscled tattooed-arms seemed steady—much steadier than Tucker's—as he aimed for blood. Tucker could see he had a perfect shot. A perfect *kill shot* to take out his eldest son.

Tucker's heart clenched and he held his breath. His eyes filled with tears as memories flooded in: Zach's purple face as he was born with the cord around his neck, and his relief when the doctor unwound it and smacked his bottom, finally getting a cry of anger in return.

Zach at Tee ball, so tired and bored in the outfield as he waited for something exciting to happen, drawing circles in the dust with a worn-out sneaker.

Zach when he ran into a tree, running uphill in the rain with his eyes closed, as they all yelled, *watch out for that tree!* from the porch, and their laughter once he'd gotten up and was okay, after nearly knocking himself out.

Such a good kid, right up until hormones and girls hit and his tongue forked, and he and Katie marveled at how fast his innocence disappeared, replaced by a back-talking, defiant young man who googled everything to prove his points.

But still... shaping up to be a fine man in spite of it all.

Or he *had been* on his way to being a fine young man.

There was no stopping it, time was flying by in fast-forward as he watched, too far away to do anything to change it.

This was *happening*.

All within a span of seconds, amid screams he now heard from his mother, Katie, too. Out of the corner of his eye, he saw she too now running in chase of her firstborn child, her mouth wide open in a strangled cry. She too saw the writing on the wall and knew she was too late.

She was going to lose her dogs *and* one of her babies.

One of *their* babies...

He cringed and squeezed his eyes shut, not wanting to see what he knew was going to happen, when all of a sudden, he heard Jake bellow.

His eyes popped up just in time to see Jake crash into Zach from atop his bike, and the two go down in a tangled mess, the wheels still spinning as the bike slid across the grass, and he could almost see the bullets whiz over their heads as Jake threw himself onto Zach, pinning the man-sized boy to ground, as the truck tore down the road and disappeared.

Tucker sank to the ground himself, dropping his gun and holding his thumping heart, his throat too tight to speak, and his legs too loose to stand.

21

TULLYMORE

TULLYMORE RAN and gathered around Jake and Zach, several lending a hand down to pull them up. Both were bleeding in several spots.

Jake stuck his hand out to Zach. "Sorry, kiddo. I didn't want to run you down with a bike, but I couldn't get your attention, and I sure as hell couldn't catch you on foot."

Zach shook his hand, not meeting his eyes, his anger apparent, but manners overriding it. Everybody knew about his and Gabby's car accident that had almost claimed Jake's life years ago, resulting in the loss of Gabby's mother. Jake still carried a few scars and a limp from it.

The boy stared down the road, biting his lip, as Katie and Tucker both arrived at the same time, panting, and nearly taking him to the ground again in a big hug from both sides, their arms wrapped tightly around him.

Katie sobbed.

Tucker stepped back and cuffed him on the head. "What were you thinking, son? Those men were shooting at you."

"They got our dogs, Dad," Zach answered through a

thick voice. "They got Hoss and Daisy. What if they hurt them?"

Tucker rubbed his son's back and looked around in confusion. "Who were they?"

Katie swiped at her eyes. "Just some guys. Four of them. Penny and I were in the garage, checking inventory on the food, when they rolled up with guns. They had us at gunpoint when Kenny, Xander, and the boys walked in. They took all our food, and when the dogs growled, they took them too. Said they'd make good fighting dogs, or—" she sucked in a huge breath and swallowed hard, "or they'd eat them."

Tucker gave a hard look to Kenny and Xander.

Both looked at the ground.

Katie defended them. "They were caught unaware, too, Tucker. They had no idea what they were walking into."

Tucker nodding, accepting it. It wasn't their fault, and they didn't have guns after all. "We need to get you two a gun." He looked back to Katie. "What's the damage? What did they get, besides Hoss and Daisy?"

"Almost everything," she answered.

His eyebrows raised. "Almost *everything*?"

"They left the heavy bags of rice and beans and a few dozen cans of vegetables, only because I'd moved a tarp over them to count the stuff that was under the tarp. They didn't see it."

The crowd murmured. This was *really* bad news. They were already short on food. How would they all eat now?

Katie looked around. "Where's Curt? Maybe we can ask him to share what they have?"

Tucker and Grayson exchanged glances.

Penny cleared her throat. "I forgot to tell you, Katie. Their food is all gone too. His wife took it all and left."

Katie looked at her in astonishment.

"Everything?" Tucker asked.

Penny nodded, her mouth a thin line.

Katie shook her head. "No. I bet Curt has more. He's probably got it hidden. Where is he? Let's ask him."

Grayson stepped up. "Curt had an accident. He's gone."

"Gone?" Katie asked. "Gone where?"

"*Gone*. As in dead. It was a bad accident."

Katie, Penny and a dozen others gasped.

Grayson looked over his shoulder and the sound of Graysie's voice. She and Puck were hurrying toward them from Neva's house, her arm around Puck. His balance seemed a bit off as they hurried toward him. "Accidental discharge. Fool shouldn't have been playing around. Y'all can bury him beside Sammi; he can keep her company. If his wife took the goods and ran, then we need to check their house. I agree with Katie...there might be more inside."

The rumble of a loud engine sounded through the neighborhood, startling everyone. The group froze and listened.

"Go!" Tucker yelled.

Everyone stood still.

"You want to get shot? Go!" he yelled again. "They're coming back!"

While people ran every which direction, heading for houses and garages, trying to find cover, Tucker gave his wife and boys a push. "Get in the house with the girls. *Hurry!* Everybody get inside and stay down. Run!"

Grayson grabbed Graysie's hand, dragging her behind him as he tried to run. She pulled back. "No, Daddy!" she yelled in panic. "Don't leave Puck!"

He skidded to a stop and looked over his shoulder. The boy just stood there, blank-faced, pulling on his pants with his free hand, his other sticking out of the sling that was across his chest, pointed at his opposite clavicle. Puck's eyeballs were doing all the work while the rest of his face and body seemed to be on break, watching everyone scatter.

"Puck! Move your dead ass and come *on*!" Grayson yelled.

"Keep going," Jake yelled at Grayson. He ran back and grabbed Puck's good arm. "Go! I got him!" He pulled a confused Puck along as they followed on Grayson and Graysie's heels, all rushing into the garage one behind the other. The kids huddled together while Jake and Grayson hunkered down under the one window to await more mayhem.

22

TULLYMORE

WITH DOZENS of eyes peeking around doors and out of windows, a convoy of military trucks rolled around the corner and stopped in front of Tucker's house. The people ran back out, excited, with hopes that the convoy had intercepted the other truck and brought their food right back.

Tucker, Jake and Grayson all hurried back out to greet them as they pulled up in front of his house. Tucker ran to the window of the Humvee, finding the same man with the scar on his face. "Hey! Did you see a box truck leave out of here a minute ago? They just robbed us."

Cutter opened the door and stepped down, putting his hands on his hips. "I didn't see anyone." Slowly, he looked out over the crowd, clicking his tongue. "Looks like you've got a lot of mouths to feed. What're you going to do now that your food is gone?"

Tucker backed up, his hand hovering over his empty gun. "I didn't say they took the food. You already knew that. You got something to do with this?"

The other men in camouflage fatigues stepped up

beside the man with the scar, sliding their rifles off their shoulders in warning.

Cutter pointed at himself. "Me? No. Why would—oh *come on*! We're just popping back in like we told you we would to offer you sanctuary. Had no *idea* you'd just been robbed, but in this day and time, there's only a few things worth dying over...and I see you finally dug your guns out of the lake," he nodded toward Tucker's waist and then looked at the heavy pistols strapped to both Grayson and Jake's sides. He looked up and around, "If they didn't take those, *and* you still have your women, it's just a lucky guess it was food they took."

Tucker's eyes narrowed, as did Jake and Grayson's, and all the eyes of his group that was now gathered around him once again. There was no doubt from the timing, and the swarmy look on the man's face, that they'd had *something* to do with this.

"Look," Cutter said. "We're not here to hurt you. We're here to help you. We did bring some news this time, too."

Tucker's hands went to his own hips. "I'm all ears."

"The grid going down has been confirmed as an attack on our country, via cyberwar. We don't have final confirmation of who it was—yet—but we know it was more than one country collaborating on it. Intel is also saying a second attack is imminent; that the grid going down was just the first phase to weaken us. I speak on behalf of the only piece of government who knows you're here: *it's not safe* to be out here on your own. There's power in numbers. Come join us at the camp and we'll all be better protected and fed."

Tucker looked out over the crowd. Unsure faces looked back at him. No one trusted these guys, but he could see the uncertainty of staying at Tullymore—especially now with very little food and water shortages—on their faces.

He looked to his own family.

Katie was flanked on either side by the girls, who each had a brother next to them, all wet-eyed and still sniffling, clung together. He knew food and water was the last thing on their minds right now. Those four-legged beasts were part of their family. They were all *very* attached to them.

"Daddy...Hoss and Daisy... We *have* to get them back," his youngest daughter begged through a broken voice, a river of tears streaming down her face.

Puck and Graysie stood behind his kids, and he watched Puck gently pat his youngest daughter's head, his own eyes filling with tears, too. The boy was nearly choking, trying not to cry out loud. He dropped his hand when he saw Tucker looking at him, and awkwardly tugged at his pants, pulling them up again, and kicking at pebble on the ground, his eyes cast down.

Tucker spoke to his group, ignoring the stranger amongst them, "If anyone wants to go, that's on you. I can't make decisions for you or your family. As for me and mine, we're staying here. I have to get our dogs back before we go anywhere."

"Was it four tattooed-up guys in a plain white box truck?" Cutter asked.

Tucker nodded emphatically. "Yeah, you know them? Where do I find them?"

Katie grabbed Tucker's arm. "They all had lots of ink, but the biggest tat that stood out was the word 'TWO' etched in barbed wire around their biceps. All four of them had that same tattoo."

Grayson and Jake exchanged a glance. They knew that mark.

Cutter shrugged. "I know *of* them. We trade with them some at the camp. If they've scavenged more food, or animals, they'll be by there. Probably soon, too. Can't promise your food arrives there—but they'll bring those dogs to the camp. You can have them back, if I have anything to say about it."

Grayson corrected the man, his voice heavy with aggression. "Scavenged hell... they *stole* that food. And damn right, the man can have his dogs back. They're *his*. Don't act like you're doing him a favor. And why do they bring you dogs? Y'all eating the pets out there?"

Cutter answered with an eye roll and then ignored Grayson, picking up a megaphone from the back of a truck. "Anybody not feel safe here? Anyone need *sanctuary*?" his voice boomed throughout the neighborhood. "FEMA's invitation is still open. Most of your community food is gone. Bad guys might come back. We can help. We have beds, shelter, and plenty of food and protection. There's rumor of an alleged second wave of attack coming on the United States, but there's safety in numbers. If you want sanctuary, *load up one bag of clothes each*. In addition, for the good of the community, you must bring whatever supplies you have on-hand. Big or small. Food or water, medicine, guns or ammo. Pack it all up, and we'll drive by each house to load it in this truck." He pointed to one of the cargo trucks. "Then we'll load you all up in this one." He pointed to the other one. "Let's get started."

Tucker and his family watched with a heavy heart as the group scattered like mice, running to and fro to gather their things. It didn't take people long to pack one bag per person, squeezing in as much as they could. Clothes, shoes, socks and armloads of pillows and blankets made their way to the truck, where people jockeyed for position on splintery wooden benches under the tarps, while the cardboard boxes of food and supplies that were carried out of the house to the curb were loaded into a different truck.

There was more food and supplies in the 'hood than he'd thought. If these people would have just thrown it all into the community pot—a new pot since their food was stolen—it may still have been possible for them all to eat for a very long time.

Soon, Katie ushered the kids into the house, united with him in his decision to stay, while he sat on the porch with Grayson, Jake, Xander and Kenny, watching the shit show.

Kenny and Xander wandered up and took a seat on the porch, and Tucker was visibly relieved to see *they* were staying. Kenny handed Tucker a bottle filled with water filtered from the pool.

As Graysie sat shoulder to shoulder with Puck off to the side, listening to the men talk, Grayson saw her reach around and soothingly rub Puck's back in big circles. The boy had fat tears rolling down his cheeks. Grayson wasn't sure if the tears were for pain from his hand from moving around so much, or if he was crying because he was just softhearted when it came to animals.

Probably crying for the dogs.

"How's your hand, boy?"

Puck wiped his nose across the back of his good hand. "It's okay, GrayMan. That woman said it wasn't infected. It doesn't hurt much," he said, though a sniffle.

So it was the dogs. Or the kids' tears, bringing down his own. The boy had a soft heart.

He shook off thoughts of Puck to give Tucker some advice. "Curt screwed more than me over when he told that gang where my farm was. The "TWO" on their arms...it stands for The Wild Ones. They might've come back here looking for the rest of their crew—two of which are six feet under. It's a biker gang on a scavenger hunt. At least they were...but you should leave, in case they come back. They don't play."

Tucker crushed the bottle of water in his hand, squirting the precious liquid out the top. "Dammit! I'm not leaving our home."

Grayson nodded. "Okay then. It looks like most of your group is abandoning ship here, man. So, if you're planning on staying, you need to fortify—and quick. Things are only going to get worse from here. Those guys are meaner'n a sack full of pissed off rattlesnakes. As soon as that convoy moves out, you need to move some cars to block the entry. Stagger them in a roadblock. Take whoever's left and have everybody move into *one* defensible home. A central command, if you will, to make your perimeter tight for focus on a smaller circle of protection. Choose one that's up on a hill with the best field of vision, preferably brick exterior."

Tucker nodded and looked to Xander and Kenny to be sure they were paying attention.

They were.

Grayson stood up, stretching his legs. "If there's any more dogs in the 'hood, bring 'em out and tie them up outside for an early defense warning. Pool whatever resources you have left. I'm sure some of the people who are staying are only doing so because they have *some* food. Also, put plywood up on the windows. Drill some gun ports in them. Fill bags with sand and stack them underneath. Make sure you have roving guards all day and all night."

Tucker nodded again at Grayson's advice, but his mind was still on the dogs. "You have a truck, Jake. You can take me to look for the dogs. At least to the camp and back. I have no idea where it is."

Jake stepped off the porch, squatted down and pulled

out a blade of grass, shredding it and watching it fall. He looked around before his eyes fell on his friend. "We don't have the fuel, man. We've got just enough in there right now to get us back to the farm. Even if we did have a full tank, where would we even start? They could be anywhere."

"But we can *start* at that camp. He said they may go there."

"And they may *not*. So say we make it to the camp... which is not a for-sure thing...how do we get you all the way back here, and then get us back to the farm? And what if those guys come back here for more? You need to take Grayson's advice and get your house in order. More bad guys out there than just them, too."

Tucker ran his hands through his shaggy hair. "Dude. I have to worry about those dogs first. I won't get a moment's peace until they're home. Katie and the kids will never forgive me if I don't get them back."

Grayson twisted his mouth, and then spit on the ground. "I guess I'm the asshole here then. And I have a dog, too: Ozzie. I love my dog. Sometimes animals are better than people. They're our family...but your real family's life is more important than a dog. Or even a couple of dogs. You may never see them again, and if you do, you might wish you hadn't—it could have already ended bad for them. Forget about *the dogs*. You need to quit majoring in the minors here. Your wife and kids come first, man."

He turned to check on his own kids, feeling horrible about what he was saying, and hoping like hell that didn't get back to Olivia. But in his heart of hearts, he knew he'd sacrifice Ozzie for either one of those kids sitting there, or Olivia, if he had to.

A look of disbelief washed over Graysie, and Puck's

lower lip trembled at his stern words as they both stared back at him with judgy eyes.

Tucker put his head in his hands and leaned over, deep in thought. "If Curt and his wife were holding out with gas in their vehicle, I bet there's others too. And there's a lot of neighbors who weren't home when the power went off and have never returned. Wherever they are, they're probably in one car. And most people have two to a couple, so I'll start checking those garages. Might be one with a full tank. It's time I scavenge their houses anyway—if Curt and Joe haven't already done it. We're going to need any food they have."

Jake stood and sighed heavily. "That's a good idea. Surprised you haven't already done it. If people aren't home yet, they may not be coming. Better you get it than someone else. You'll share with whoever's left here. But about the dogs...Grayson's right, buddy. Forget about saving the dogs. Family first—and on that note, I'm worried about ours. We've got to head back to the farm now."

23

THE FARM

"HERE." Jake tossed Grayson the keys. "You drive."

Puck and Graysie climbed into the back of Ruby, with a stern warning from Grayson to sit on their butts with the cab at their back. Grayson checked Graysie's rifle while she checked Puck's pistol. He handed the rifle back to her with a wink, watched Puck carefully holster his own gun, and then they drove out of Tullymore, the road unfolding before them in a hurry to get home.

The streets were barren, other than random cars that must've ran out of gas, left to gather rust and rodents on the side of the road. It was an urban desert devoid of all life. It wasn't uncommon not to pass anyone on the backroad they'd taken even *before* the grid went down, thus they hadn't been surprised to not see a soul on the way to Tullymore. Luckily, it looked like they might not see anyone on the way home either.

Or maybe not so luckily.

Grayson wondered where all the people had gone. *This is eerie.*

Jake pulled a notepad out of the glove box and soon, a

pencil was rapidly scratching on paper, while Grayson chose his own route home, a different and normally busier road than the one that'd brought them to Tullymore. "What're you writing?" he asked Jake.

"Drawing Tucker a map to that camp. We'll check on the girls, then see how much gas we have. If both are okay, then I'll go back and give this to him. Maybe even drive him there," he said, lowering his voice on the last sentence.

"Jake," Grayson said somberly. "I don't like that idea. We've been mostly lucky so far. Let's not push it. Besides, yeah...you may be able to squeeze out enough good gas for one more tank, but what if *we* need it? You can't be a hero to everyone."

Jake stopped drawing. "I'm not trying to be a hero. He's my *friend*, Grayson. I already feel like I abandoned him by not staying in Tullymore when I know he needed my help there. I can at least *try* to help him get his dogs back."

Grayson bit his lip in thought. "I don't want to pull rank here, but that gas is mine. The truck *is* yours though...but, if it was me, I'd rather walk there and save the gas. That camp is only about ten miles from the farm by road. Closer if we cut through pastures and woods." He glanced at the rear-view mirror, seeing Puck's face shoved into the slide window, half in the cab now, listening with interest to their conversation.

"Puck, *sit down* with your back against the cab, like I already told you." He gently chided, pushing Puck's face backward and sliding the window closed with his right hand. He continued with Jake, "Your place is with your wife. Sorry, brutha, but family trumps friends and neighbors."

Jake sighed and folded his map, sticking it into the note-book and slamming the cover over it. He shoved it into the glove box, crossed his arms and leaned back with his head against the glass, his eyes closed in thought.

Grayson turned a corner. "Jake, look at this."

The road they were on was a rural road, populated once with nice little homes that each sat on a half-acre of land, all in a pretty row, one beside the other for miles. But the houses had been consumed by fires. The road was now nothing more than a long line of blackened stone and burnt dreams, where it had once housed dozens of families.

Grayson slowed down to get a better look, now noticing the almost dissipated cloud of smoke that still hung low in the air. "What do you think happened? Power lines? Maybe a transformer exploded?"

Jake stared at the window. "No. Can't be that. The lines are *underground* on this—shit! Grayson, stop the truck. There's a man back there in the ditch, on my side."

Grayson slid the back-window open and issued orders to Graysie and Puck. "Both of you slide to my side of the truck and have your guns ready."

He slammed on brakes and reversed. "Wait," he said to Jake. "Get your gun out and hold it on him for a minute or two. This might be a trick."

The engine rumbled quietly as they slid up beside the guy and stopped, seeing right away he wouldn't be pulling any tricks on anyone from the mad rush of feathers flying up when they scared off two carrion birds intent on cleaning the bones of the already bloated man.

Graysie yelled from the back, "Daddy, *go*!" He turned and stole a glance at her, seeing her cover her nose and mouth with one hand, while firmly gripping her rifle in the other. His head on a swivel, he checked for other danger around them, but seeing no one, realized it was the smell of the body roasting in the heat that she wanted to run from.

Jake jumped out of the truck to get a better look.

"We'll go in a second, Graysie. Watch Jake's six," Grayson yelled back to her.

Jake approached the man and called out, getting no answer. Just in case, he gently pushed on his leg with the toe of his boot and was met with a wet-sucking sound as he dislodged the body, causing it to roll a bit further into the ditch. Buzzing flies took flight, then returned to hang like a halo over the corpse's head. It took only a moment and Jake was hurrying back into the truck. "He's got a bullet hole in his back. Let's get out of here."

Grayson waited for Graysie to sit and then put the pedal to the metal, speeding to the next corner and taking a swift right, swerving on the gravel straight into the path of a crowd of desperate and hungry people—the rabble immediately raising arms and yelling at them to stop as several dove for the truck.

24

THE FARM

GRAYSON SKIDDED TO A STOP, inches from the first two women in a crowd of more than fifty, the milling mob making it impossible to go forward.

They pushed forward, ten deep in front of the truck and moving to the sides.

Several voices rang out.

"Give us a ride!"

"Do you have food?"

"I need water!"

"Help us!"

Graysie hurried a frightened Puck to the middle of the bed of the truck, away from the desperate reaching arms as the horde closed in, trying to climb their way into the truck. She pushed them back with the butt of her rifle, frantically running from one side to the other. "Daddy, put it in reverse! Hurry!"

Grayson frantically looked around, hoping for a clear path. The eyes on these people—empty of reason, and full of hunger. This was going to end badly. "Shoot them, Jake!"

Rough hands pulled at the passenger door, opening it a

crack. Jake grabbed it and slammed it shut again, hitting the door lock with a closed fist. "Hell no, we can't just *shoot* innocent people," he answered, pushing another set of hands off his window sill.

Grayson snatched a glance at the kids, seeing Puck cowering in the middle of the truck bed, scared and overwhelmed by the crowd, he had his arms wrapped around his knees and his eyes squeezed tightly shut while Graysie fought them off of three sides alone, running back and forth.

"Dammit, Jake! That's my kids back there! Spring those fuckers a leak if they get in!"

He slammed into reverse, and took off like a shot, knocking two people to the ground, and feeling a *thu-wump* as the wheels rolled over one. "Get down, Graysie!" he yelled, and waited half a second as Graysie fell to the bed of the truck and wrapped her arms around Puck, hanging on for dear life.

Grayson whipped the truck backward into a turn, putting them back on the road with the burnt-down houses, and reversed their trail, running Ruby like a scalded dog, and hoping her old parts would stick together, all the way home.

Upon arrival, he skidded to a stop in front of the house, with steam still coming out of his ears. He jumped from the truck and tore into Puck. "Listen here, Puck. The next time you hunker down while a girl protects your big ass, you can turn in that gun. *Do you hear me*?"

Puck cowered in the truck, his chin quivering, and Graysie put a protective arm around him. "Daddy! He was scared."

"We're *all* scared!" Grayson roared. "And I'm talking to *Puck*! You mind your own business, girl. *Get in the house*," his voice thundered. He jabbed a finger toward the door, where Olivia and Gabby were standing with wide eyes, Ozzie between them.

The dog tucked tail and hid behind Olivia.

Graysie squeezed Puck's hand and climbed out of the truck, throwing angry glances over her shoulder at her father.

Jake stepped out of the truck and bit his lip, his eyes falling to the ground.

Grayson took a deep breath. "Get outta the truck, boy."

Puck chuffed, trying to swallow down a sob, as he awkwardly climbed down using only one hand—the other still secure in his sling. He stood with his head hung low, his own eyes on his feet, tugging at his pants nervously with one hand.

"Boy, quit yankin' at your drawers. You've got a belt now," Grayson muttered irritably. He wasn't so mad that Puck didn't protect Graysie—he knew when it came down to it, the boy would pull and shoot to defend the women. He'd already proven that.

Grayson was *scared*. Scared that if no one else was around, Puck wouldn't defend *himself*. The boy was selfless, and that was a quality that Grayson admired in him, but he needed to buck up for himself as well.

He couldn't stand to lose this kid, when he'd just found him.

Puck dropped his one good hand to his side to hang limply and swallowed hard. "I'm sorry, GrayMan."

Grayson exhaled.

"Look, Puck. I *know* you're brave. I've seen it. Several times now. You stayed all alone at Mama Dee's when you were scared of the dark, and risked my wrath by stealing from my garden to make sure Jenny didn't starve. You battled a hive of bees to try to get honey to feed our family. You even took on Trunk's gang, and killed two men. That's bravery. We might *all* be dead if it weren't for you."

Puck didn't respond.

"Puck, look at me."

Puck's watery eyes wandered up, but he looked through Grayson, refusing to meet his eyes, his chin still quivering.

Grayson continued, "But when it comes to protecting *yourself*, you choke. Remember when I first found you up in that tree where those boys chased you? You're big enough you could'a whipped *all* of them boys. And just *now*, that mob could've dragged you out of that truck. Graysie too. There was too many for Graysie to fight off. You hunkered down and closed your eyes to it. If they'd have got you, then Graysie would've jumped out to save you, the same as you would her. I just need you to stand up for yourself, okay?"

Puck nodded, lobbing a fast-running tear off his cheek.

"Stop crying," Grayson admonished. This was new world and it had no room for tears. As much as it pained him to hurt Puck's feelings, the boy was going to have to toughen up.

Puck nodded again, and swiped at his face. "Sorry. Can me and Jenny still stay here with you, Grayman? I'll try to do better. I don't want you to not like me."

Silence engulfed Grayson and he had to swallow hard. He coughed and caught his brother-in-law's disappointed eyes before Jake turned around and stomped up the steps, slamming the screen door behind him. Olivia and Gabby followed, punctuating their feelings with a repeat of the slamming door, leaving Grayson alone with the boy, other than the judging eyes of Ozzie that stayed glued on them from the safety of the porch.

Grayson rushed in and grabbed Puck, bringing him to

close to his chest, smothering the boy in a tight hug. "Listen here, Puck. I don't *like* you," he whispered, not able to bring his thick voice any louder. "I *love* you, kid. I'm sorry...and you ain't going *nowhere*, you hear me? We're your family now. I won't turn you away just for making a mistake. I won't turn you away *at all*," he said, his voice breaking on the last two words. "You're my boy now," he whispered.

Puck reached around with his good arm and hugged Grayson back, tears of relief now flowing freely. "Thank you, Grayman. But I'll do better next time. You'll see. I'll be tough like Graysie," he said, clinging to the older man.

Grayson stepped back from Puck, straightened up and swiped away a sneaky tear. He cleared his throat. "That's right. You'll toughen up," he said, and gave Puck a firm nod.

25

THE FARM

GRAYSON STOOD ALONE at the truck now, surrounded only by a chatter of obnoxious chickens who had listened to his tearful confession to Puck with no interest.

Puck had wandered off to find more solace with Jenny. He could already picture the big lug's arms around the donkey's neck, burying his angelic face in the burro's hair. Just that morning he had gifted her with a paracord harness that he'd braided himself, eager to present for her appreciation, as though it were the finest piece of jewelry. She'd snorted at it, but indulged the boy when he'd fitted it on, seeming right at ease with it.

Jenny had become more tolerant of Puck's affections in the past few weeks. Grayson supposed it was because he was the one familiar thing to her in a world that had gone upside-down. It wasn't unusual for Puck to have hour-long conversations with her, hugging her neck to make each point, and lavishing affection upon her.

She in turn followed him everywhere, like a very tall dog, even seemingly jealous when Puck threw the ball for Ozzie. If it happened to land near her, she'd snatch it up between her big square teeth and seemingly tease Ozzie with it while he sat obediently in front of her—just as he did the humans—hopeful eyes looking up, sloppy tongue lolling out in wait. But she disappointed him time and time again with one big crunch, rudely dropping the remains of his ball at his feet.

Every. Single. Time.

The ass was heartless to the dog.

Luckily, the church had no need for tennis balls, leaving a full tote of them out in the container, unmolested by Olivia.

And now it was time to face Olivia...

Dragging his feet, he made his way into the house to face the music, and stopped short just inside the door, his mouth in a hushed "O" of surprise.

Upon his couch, Olivia was nestled between two small children, telling them a story...

"—Once upon a time, there lived a mean man on a farm, and his name was Mr. Marshall Mellow. But the man wasn't *really* mean. People just *thought* he was, because he wore a cranky look on his face, and said *snappy grouchy* words when he tried to hide his real feelings to make everyone believe he was the toughest guy in the world. But you see, the mean man was *really* a marshmallow inside—just a little burnt around the edges. If you bit in deep enough though, he was sweet..."

She looked up at her husband with a glare.

"Me and Puck made up," Grayson said, his hands in his pockets.

"You make it sound like it was a fair fight," Olivia answered, and then pursed her lips.

Gabby and Jake, cuddled together on the loveseat, raised matching eyebrows, and then looked at the floor.

Grayson sighed. "I said I was sorry to the kid. But you don't know what we went through out there. It was some scary shit. He's got to toughen up."

"Watch your language," she admonished him, with a glance at the kids. "And I do know. Jake and Graysie told me." Olivia stood up and hugged her husband and then stood back and waved an arm toward the children. "Honey, meet Briar and Brody. They're going to be living with us."

The skinny boy closed the gap that Olivia had left between them, scooting over and putting a protective arm around his little sister. The little girl looked at Grayson with wide, scared eyes and then hid her face on her brother's chest.

Grayson felt a familiar vein ticking in his forehead and he looked at the ceiling. He blew out a breath. "Olivia, can I see you in the bedroom?"

Olivia waved Graysie over to the couch and gave the children a quick smile as her husband stomped from the living room. She followed closely on his heels.

"I can explain," she said as she shut their bedroom door. "Sit down."

Grayson sat heavily on the bed, his head in his hands. "Tell me."

"Gabby and I found them."

"They're not stray dogs, Olivia. We can't keep them."

"Grayson...listen," she pleaded, and then told him the story of their meth-head mother and the two men who wanted to get their hands, literally, on the little girl. She explained they'd scared the two men with stories of trigger-happy husbands, one of which was a law enforcement officer, and the other which was DEA—a drug enforcement officer; neither of which was true. The men had ridden off into the sunset with a promise to never return, taking the woman, who seemed giddy with excitement to be kid-free, with them.

Grayson shook his head. "Olivia, we don't have enough *food*."

She sat down on the bed beside him, putting her hand on his leg. "We'll make due. We found a ton of Prickly Pear Cactus out there, all of them at least waist high, at least a dozen or more. And dandelions, and a few berry bushes. I'm sure there's all sorts of other things. We just have to look." She picked up her wild foraging book from the bedside table and flipped through, showing Grayson a half dozen plants she'd circled with notes on where around the property they'd found it. "And Elmer said he'd hunt for meat. Tina and Tarra are closing in on those wild hogs, too."

"That's still not enough. Children need more than that. They need milk, and vitamins, and...well, all sorts of things we don't have or even know about anymore. These kids are a liability."

Olivia stood up, her hands on her hips. "Grayson Rowan, you will *not* call those kids a liability. They're innocent children! And they have nowhere else to go. They'll stay here with us, and if we don't have enough food, they can have mine," she finished, stamping her foot. "Now you get yourself together, *Mr. Marshall Mellow*, and then come back out here and greet these babies with a smile, or so help me..."

She stomped out of the bedroom, leaving the last words unsaid, and a chuckle dying to get out of Grayson. It wasn't often she stomped her foot or crossed swords with him. But when she did, she meant it.

He closed his eyes and sighed.

But the food...

His anger came rushing back.

Of course they can have your food...Olivia...you've given most of our food away already, why wouldn't you give them what's left?! He smashed his fist into the mattress, finally venting his frustration with his wife.

And then he pushed that thought out of his head and reminded himself that this *was* the woman he'd married. It was nothing new. She was the heart in their marriage and he had no doubt she'd meant what she said. She'd *starve* before taking food from a child's mouth.

And he'd starve right along with her.

It wasn't even a question. He might grumble about it, but he wasn't a total monster. He couldn't put two innocent children out, or take them back to that mess they were found in —and Olivia damn well knew it.

But he felt justified to get a little bent about it, at least.

He stood and rubbed his jaw, now aching worse than ever, and convinced a fake, stiff smile to appear before going to meet the two newest additions to his ever-growing family.

26

THE FARM

As NIGHT FINALLY FELL, a small blaze burned in the fire pit, battling the mosquitos, while the family gathered nearby at the two picnic tables—one hastily built today to accommodate all of them. Puck and Jake had pushed the tables end to end so they could all eat together.

For now.

Sautéed Dandelion greens steamed from their plates, with a generous helping of rabbit stew over rice, compliments of Elmer, freshly hunted and skinned, and deliciously cooked in his solar oven, using the Fresnel lens. A side of cool, sliced cucumbers and tomatoes from the garden topped off their meal.

Tomorrow would be a busy day. With even more people under his roof, Grayson had assigned designated sleeping arrangements: he, Olivia and Ozzie would sleep in the master bedroom. Gabby and Jake would have the spare. Graysie was in her own room, where she would share her double bed with Briar and Brody. Tina and Tarra would sleep in the pop-up camper, which the ladies had managed to get clean and ready today in his absence. Elmer would sleep on the couch, and Puck would sleep in their small basement. It was only a fourth the size of the house—positioned directly under the two spare bedrooms—but dry and mostly without varmints. It'd do fine for Puck to have a little bit of room.

Puck wasn't too happy with his assignment, complaining that Jenny wouldn't have a window to talk to him through. Grayson—and everybody else—knew that wasn't the only reason; he was scared to sleep down there alone. So, it was no surprise when Elmer claimed the couch was lumpy and that he'd rather sleep downstairs with Puck.

Puck was grinning ear to ear. He absolutely loved Elmer.

Elmer beamed. He loved the boy right back. "I'd imagine that flea bag dog will be down there with us too," he grumbled, and winked at Puck.

Puck smiled even wider. He adored Ozzie and loved it when the dog curled up next to him. He thought no one knew he'd been luring the dog from Grayson and Olivia's bedroom with a treat each night.

Grayson patted Puck on the back. "Boy, you look like a mule eating briars over there grinning like that. Since you seem so happy now with your sleeping assignment, I'll tell you the bad news. You have to clean it out and organize it."

Puck shrugged, never begrudging any chore. "Okay. What do I do?"

"You'll find a mess down there, but Graysie's going to help you since you have one bum hand. Start by clearing the floor. You can stack as many totes and boxes as you can on the shelves. Put the long-term storage food buckets under the stairs. Stack the porta-toilet and all the paper products on top of those, and if you run out of room, take some stuff to the barn. There's a leak in the container and until I get it fixed, I don't want to put anything else in there. I've been putting it off, but hopefully we'll beat the rain," he explained.

"What am I going to sleep on, GrayMan?"

"On the shelf, you'll find three blow-up mattresses and some pillows and bedding in shrink-wrap plastic. Olivia bought those for the teenagers at church to use during lock-ins. Blow up two. One for you, and one for Elmer."

Puck looked at him in surprise. "Your church locks in their teenagers? *Why?*"

Everybody laughed. Even Briar and Brody, who had been silent as mice, giggled.

"No. I mean, yes. They do lock them in. But they *want* to be locked in. It's sorta like a slumber party for older kids."

"Oh, can I go? I've always wanted to go to a slumber party!"

The adults exchanged sad looks.

"Sure you can," Grayson said, and smiled. "As soon as things are straightened out with the power, we'll take you."

Puck nodded and happily dug into his food.

Jake swallowed a bite of rabbit stew, and wiped his mouth. "What's on the agenda for the rest of us?"

Grayson forked a red, ripe tomato and looked out over his newly extended family. He popped it into his mouth and chewed, deep in thought.

First priority was to *protect* them.

"You and I are going to be felling trees. It's time to fortify here. After seeing that crowd walking last night—even though they weren't headed in this direction, *yet*—we need to make sure we can protect this place. I've been thinking on it, and I think we need to camouflage the driveway. We'll crisscross trees at the road, blocking it from view and access, and make tall piles of brush all alongside before and after it. Maybe people won't even see the farm, and walk on by. We can use the tractor, and Elmer, you're running that while Jake and I play lumberjack. When we don't need you, I want you start on digging a trench all the way around the house. One big square, and include the barn, the container, and the camper in it. I'll explain what to do with that later."

Tina waved her hand. "What about us little women? Not all of us are helpless," she said with a wink toward Olivia.

Olivia rolled her eyes.

Grayson laughed. "Didn't think you were. But if you insist, then sure. Next thing is to dig some foxholes around the perimeter of the house."

"Foxholes?" Tarra asked. "For what?"

"To hide in. To take cover in. To shoot from...See those *huge* potted plants lining the driveway?" He pointed at the pots, each containing the remains of an ornamental tree. No one had paid much attention to them since the power had gone off as they had more important plants to worry about —like the garden. "We need six holes about the diameter of those pots. Leave the dead trees in them. I'll mark the spots. Dig them big enough, and deep enough, for a man to get on his knees with a rifle, and not get his head blown off. I'll mount some old wheels on pallets to set the pots on, and we'll paint them to match the pots. We can roll them out of the way when we need the foxholes."

Neither Tina nor Tarra blinked an eye. Both were more than capable of doing some digging, and would most likely be the first *man* in the hole, if and when the shooting started.

Grayson continued, "Don't try to move the pots when you're done. I want to see each hole, try it on for size, and then put some supplies in each one; ammo and stuff. Plus, it'll take more than the two of you to lift them onto the pallets. They're extremely heavy. Jake and I will help with that."

"What if Emma and Dusty make it home? How are they going to drive past the trees and avoid the foxholes to get to the house?" Olivia asked.

Emma was Gabby and Olivia's little sister who had taken off to Bald Head Island, North Carolina almost three weeks ago, on a bicycle, going after her son and husband who were stranded there, when the grid went down. Her husband was Grayson's little brother, Dusty. They'd heard no word from them yet...

Grayson shrugged. "They'll find their way in. The foxholes will be covered unless we need them, and if we *need* them, I doubt Dusty and Emma would pop in during a firefight," he explained, patting his wife on the hand. "Stop worrying about Emma. She's a big girl now. Next, we need to relocate some of those Prickly Pear Cacti. I want them planted under as many windows as we can. It'll be tough for anyone to get through those things without some sort of body armor, head to toe. Plus, we'll have them close by to eat."

He waved his fork at all of the ladies. "I also need your help in making the inside of the house more secure. I'm going to be nailing plywood to the inside of the windows and drilling shooting holes in them, but in the meantime, look in the barn for burlap feed bags. If you can't find enough, get the big, black Hefty garden trash bags and double-bag them...maybe even triple-bag them. Then set one in front of each window. You're going to use the dirt that comes out of the fox-holes to fill those bags. If you need more, steal it from the berm behind the gun range. Use a shovel and wheelbarrow and transfer it into those bags in the house."

"Dirt inside?" Oliva sneered. "For *what*?"

"For protection from bullets flying into the house," Grayson answered quietly, wishing the children weren't hanging on their every word. "I'd much rather have dirt on the floor than lead in our ass."

Olivia scoffed. "Seriously, Grayson? Don't you think you're overdoing it a bit? It's not *that bad* out there yet."

How easily she'd forgotten her trip home from Myrtle Beach. The gang, the weirdos, Mei, the desperate refugees camped at the rest area, the men who jumped Elmer and Emma, and the bloodbath that her little sister was responsible for that followed...

Her answer was a dead-stare reaction from every adult who'd been 'out there.'

27

THE FARM

THAT NIGHT, Graysie spoke in a low voice, in the dark. "Once upon a time, there was a very, very poor boy," she said. "The boy was wandering in the deep, dark forest looking for food for his family because he had no money. Suddenly, he found a beautiful magic mushroom—but his mama had told him to never, ever eat mushrooms. They could be *dangerous*. But he was so hungry that he picked it up anyway, when a tiny group of fierce fairies appeared and blew on the mushroom, so that he couldn't take a bite, and it turned to dust, leaving two gold coins in his hand..."

Puck lay cramped and miserable in the space between the bed and the window on Graysie's bedroom floor, his hand throbbing. Ozzie was spread out beside him, all four feet in the air, while Graysie cuddled a child on each side of her—the *littles*, as GrayMan called them. He and Graysie were 'the kids,' and Briar and Brody were the 'Littles,' because GrayMan said they were *all* kids and it was confusing.

Briar and Brody were homesick for their mother, and restless. She couldn't read the books anymore because

GrayMan said they had to turn out the lantern to save the batteries, so she was making up the stories, trying to get the little kids to nod off.

She finished the story about the mushroom, ending with the boy buying all sorts of yummy food for his family, and then paused to take a deep, exhausted breath before starting into a rhyme. "Ten little monkeys, jumping on the bed—"

"—Graysie?" Puck interrupted, from the floor.

"What?"

"How am I gonna count to ten now?"

"What do you mean?"

"I don't have ten fingers," he whispered, holding both his hands up in the dark, where only he could see.

There was a long pause. "You still have *part* of that finger. Now you just have *three* pinkies. So, you can still count to ten, Puck. It's no big deal. It's sorta cool."

Puck thought about GrayMan's ring. He loved that ring. And GrayMan could never get another. When GrayMan had given it to him, Puck had asked him if they both could have one so that they'd have matching rings. Grayman had said, *Nope. It's one of a kind, boy*, and he'd given it *him* for safekeeping.

GrayMan had trusted him with his ring.

He felt awful that he'd lost it. Maybe he could find it again, like the boy in the forest who'd found the magic mushroom... *that* boy was a hero. And like Graysie in the back of the truck, fighting off the bad people who tried to get in. She'd protected him.

Girls can be heroes too, he thought.

If he found the ring, GrayMan *and* the little kids would see *he* was a hero, too.

"Graysie?" Puck whispered again. "Can I sleep up there? I'm not comfy."

"No, Puck. There's not room. You'll have a bed tomorrow in the basement. Go to sleep."

Puck sighed. "I want to hear the stories, too," he whined.

She shifted in the bed. "You can hear the stories from there, Puck, if you be quiet."

Puck blew out a frustrated breath and rolled over on the hard floor. He already knew the ending anyway. They were all the same. Each one had a hero. The hero saved something or somebody. Or they found something special that brought something even more special.

Puck wanted to be a hero more than anything. He thought back to earlier and realized GrayMan might not still be mad at him, but he *didn't* think he was a hero. More like a scaredy-cat. Probably everybody did.

Bang, bang, bang

Someone beat on the door.

Grayson jumped from the bed, grabbing his shot gun and a flashlight at the same time as Jake jumped from his bed, pulling his pistol from the holster on his bedside table, and grabbing the battery-operated lantern.

They met at the door, behind Tina and Tarra who hadn't moved into the camper just yet, and were already in position on either side of it, their pistols pointed safely at the ceiling, but held close to their chests. Elmer sat on the couch in rumpled clothes, wide awake and hunkered over with his own shotty pointed at the door, the moonlight reflecting off his half-bald head.

Grayson waved his gun down. "Don't point it at me, Elmer...I've got to open the door!"

"Then move outta the way, boy," Elmer grumbled.

Grayson shook his head at the old timer and leaned his shoulder against the door. "Who is it?" he roared loudly.

"It's Nick."

Grayson waved the guns down and swung the door open. He stepped past Nick and looked out around the yard. Finally, satisfied Nick was alone, he turned to him on the porch. "What the hell drug you all the way out here, to the middle of nowhere in the middle of the night?" he grumbled.

"I see you're in fine spirits, Grayson. Nice to see you alive, too."

Nick was the owner of QualPro Auto & Marine, a local repair shop that shared property with a used car and marine dealership, and the place where Jake and Grayson both took their vehicles for service. He didn't look any worse for wear...still the same short salt and pepper colored beard and closely-trimmed hair. Skinny, as usual, but not any skinner than usual.

Jake stepped up and shook Nick's hand. "Good to see you, buddy."

Nick had saved Jake's life. Or so he claimed. When Jake lost his shit at the sight of a man taking a bullet, Nick took the credit—or the blame—for shooting the man who'd pulled Jake off the four-wheeler to steal it.

Without Nick there, pushing him to flee, Jake would surely have stayed to pay the piper, and faced the mob of the man's buddies that were running toward him. He may have never made it to the farm to meet up with Gabby when the lights first went out.

He owed Nick.

"Where's Rena?" Jake asked.

"She's gone, man."

Jake felt like the air was pushed out of him. "Oh man. I'm so sorry."

Nick laughed at Jake's stricken face. "No, she's not dead. I'm sure she's fine. I meant she took off. Good riddance, I say. One less mouth to feed."

Jake laughed in relief. The two had always had a volatile on-again, off-again relationship, which would make things even worse in the apocalypse. They loved hard, but they fought hard too. It was both their faults; two peas in a pod. But Rena was a nice girl and he hoped she was doing okay out there.

Grayson grumpily waved him in, stepping over Tina and Tarra's blankets all over the floor, and sat down, still holding his gun. "So I'll ask again...what brings you here?"

Nick harrumphed at Grayson. "Damn man, that's a fine way to say thank you."

"Thank you for what?"

"Some gang came out to the shop. Knocked us around a bit looking for Olivia and Gabby. I didn't tell them anything, and I guess they didn't find you. A little thank you, maybe?"

"They found us," Grayson answered tersely, wiping off his gun with his T-shirt.

Nick's eyes got wide. "Not by me they didn't. I swear. I even knocked out one of my guys so he didn't run his mouth. Popped him in the noggin with a wrench. They left knowing *nothing*."

Jake patted Nick on the shoulder. "Thanks, man. We know it wasn't by you. Had a rat at Tullymore that told them. They're gone now, though. So is the rat. Don't worry about it."

"Oh yeah, that's the other reason I came out here. I went there first to warn you, in case you were there, and because I passed right by it, and Tullymore is on *fire*, man. Big time. Whopping huge flames shooting straight up to the sky!"

"Wait. What?" Jake asked in disbelief. His knees wobbled and he sat heavily in a chair. "Is everybody okay? What about my house?"

"Your house is gone, dude. *Gone.*" He snapped his fingers. "Nothing left but charcoal and kindling now."

Jake ran his hands over his face. Tina and Tarra sat down on the couch with Elmer. Grayson waved Nick to a chair too and went into the kitchen to fetch two glasses of water, one for Nick and one for Jake.

"Tucker and Katie...and the kids?" Jake asked hopefully. "Kenny and Xander? Their families? Everybody okay?"

Nick sadly shook his head. "They're gone, too."

Gabby stumbled into the room, having heard the conversation from the hallway but in her nightgown and not wanting to step into the room with Nick. "No," she cried, running to Jake. Jake caught her and brought her down easy into the chair with him.

Nick stood up suddenly. "No, Gabby! I'm so sorry. I mean they're *gone*.... not *dead*. They took off with the rest of the folks from Tullymore in the back of military cargo trucks. I watched everything from the woods."

Gabby wiped away her tears. "Oh. Well, that's good then, right?"

Jake nodded. "Yeah. That's good. It must've been the same guys from the FEMA camp. Guess they had to accept their help after all. At least they're safe." He squeezed her hand and gave her a weak smile, his heart still beating a song of thunder at the bad news.

Grayson shook his head and sat down. "Bullshit. Ain't nothing sound good about that story. That's more screwed up than a blonde's checkbook."

Nick accepted the glass of water that Grayson handed him and drank deeply before answering. He sat the glass down and wiped his mouth, then shook his head. "You'd be right, Grayson. That's what I was coming to warn you about when I went by Tullymore. Rumor is those weren't *real* military trucks. Those asshats came through town stealing food and supplies, and then later setting homes on fire themselves, so that they could *rescue* people," he held up his fingers to put quotes around the word rescue, "but some say they're really militia gone rogue. I was coming here to warn you not to go with them. Tucker and his family, and everyone else from Tullymore, could be in deep shit."

"Can they leave if they want to?" Jake asked.

Nick shrugged. "I have no idea. I haven't seen hide nor hair of anyone coming *back*, that had said they were going. For all we know, it might be a five-star resort there. At least we know they have food and shelter."

Grayson frowned. "Actually, we *don't* know that."

Jake squeezed Gabby's hand and pierced Grayson with a heavy stare, which Grayson avoided.

A pregnant lull filled the room. He knew what they were asking. "We worry about our own place first. Follow the plan first thing tomorrow morning to fortify the farm, and then, we'll go check on your friends. Deal?"

Jake blew out a held breath and nodded. "Deal."

28

THE FARM

PUCK TRIED out his new bed in the basement—just a mattress on the floor—and took a moment to stretch out and stare at the ceiling. He listened to the rumble of the tractor outside. Everyone was working out there, except him and Graysie—and the Littles. They'd been stuck in the basement most of the day, just recently finishing up their project.

He picked up his sketch pad and crayons and considered drawing what was in his head, but decided not to. Olivia and Gabby didn't seem to like his pictures, staring at them a long time and whispering when they thought he wasn't listening.

He put his things down.

He was bored. He rolled over to look at the now-neat shelf that Graysie had helped him organize. One row of jars with pretty-colored food took up a whole shelf. Graysie had moved those so they didn't get broken. On the bottom shelf, cases of water, food buckets, and two totes were tidily stacked, and on the other two shelves, toilet paper and more totes. Everything was now off the floor, other than the big roll of plastic sheeting still leaned against the corner, and a long green garden hose, all wound up in a pile on the floor.

Graysie said to carry that out to the barn. It was too big to fit into the space they had left.

He eyeballed the rest of the stuff. Lots of things he didn't understand. One box had a picture of a stove, with a pot filled with food. Did the box have a *stove* in it? Or was it a box of pots? Or was it *that food* on the picture? Because *that* food looked *really* good and Puck wanted to eat it.

But Graysie kept saying, *not now, Puck,* and went too fast for his questions. She had no time for *him* now. She wanted to get back to the *Littles.*

He'd found funny white suits in one box with silver tape and face masks. He'd stepped into a suit and held a mask over his face, but it had scared Briar and Brody so badly that they'd run upstairs. Graysie got mad at him and made him take if off. She didn't want to play dress-up.

She was *no fun* anymore.

She did explain the portable toilet, and it made him laugh, thinking of GrayMan sitting on it to poop. He'd look pretty silly.

Graysie said they were supposed to be *working.* To stop playing. So he helped blow up two mattresses, and now his head felt woozy. Elmer's mattress lay just a few feet away from his, separated by a small table holding a lantern. Both were the same, with a sheet, a blanket and a pillow, but Elmer's bed was special.

Puck had found a ragged, old teddy bear in Graysie's closet and put it on his pillow.

He knew Elmer was still sad, and he'd told Puck that he'd lay down there but couldn't promise he'd sleep much. He explained that he hadn't slept alone in a bed, without his wife, for more years than Puck was alive.

Elmer was *old...*

Puck hoped he would name his new bear, 'Edith,' or maybe "Edie."

Now he was pouting that Graysie had said no to his *best* idea. Even though he'd said *after* they were done *working*... she still said *no*. He'd wanted to unroll the big roll of plastic, and squirt some soap on it and make a slide for *all of them* to play on. Briar and Brody would like that, he just knew it. But Graysie said GrayMan would get mad because it was *prepping stuff*, and he probably had a plan for it, and she said they couldn't waste the soap either.

Briar and Brody didn't want to play with him anyway. It made Puck sad. They looked at him funny. They were afraid of him. Graysie said to not stand over them too close. She said to them, he looked like a giant. So he got down on his knees to talk to them, but they still looked at him funny. He wasn't gonna hurt them. He only wanted to have fun and share his new family with them, but they just didn't like him.

And, they were stealing *all* Graysie and Olivia's time.

Graysie was upstairs with them right now, telling them *more* stories, and reading them books while the grownups worked outside. Puck didn't want to listen anymore. Graysie had already read him all those stories over and over before the Littles came. Every story was the same.

The hero.

All they wanted to hear about was how *brave* the hero was.

Like he *hadn't* been yesterday.

He gathered up the garden hose and carried it up the narrow basement stairs, passing them once again as he went outside. He sighed, and threw a begrudged look over his shoulder at the two of them cuddled beside Graysie on the couch, smiling and pointing at the pictures in a book, while she read.

He stepped onto the porch and looked around the farm. It was a flurry of activity. GrayMan said it was even more important to get the farm ready.

But ready for what? Puck thought.

Tina and Tarra were digging holes in the front yard. Olivia and Gabby had on silly, thick gloves and were replanting pokey things under a window, and Elmer was driving the tractor, carrying a huge load of downed trees toward the road.

Ozzie ran up and dropped a tennis ball at his feet, grinning from ear to ear at Puck's arrival. Puck rubbed the dog's head and threw the ball, having to juggle the hose against chest to do it. It didn't go far, and Ozzie brought it right back.

"Sorry, boy. Today's a work-day..." Puck mumbled. He hurried over to Tina and Tarra, with Ozzie on his heels. "I want to do something brave," he blurted out to the two ladies.

They stopped digging and exchanged a raised brow.

Tina leaned on her shovel. "Like what, Puck?"

"I don't know. Something really brave."

She shrugged. "I think you were brave when you protected everyone from those bad guys here. You were *very* brave then." Tina stabbed the shovel into the dirt, continuing her project.

"But everybody already forgot that. I need to do something *else*. I want to be a hero."

Puck stomped his foot, and Ozzie dropped his ball, looking up at the boy with pleading eyes. Puck scooted the ball over with his foot, giving the dog a silent no. He didn't want to admit it, but his hand really did hurt. He didn't feel like throwing a ball today.

Tarra crawled out of the fox hole and leaned against her own shovel. "That's not true. No one will ever forget your bravery that day. See, *we* remembered. Right? You'll always be a brave hero after that. So how about being a *helpful* hero now? Lots of work going on here today..."

Puck screwed his lips to the side in thought. "I was helpful. I helped Graysie clean up the basement. I want to be brave now."

Tina looked over her shoulder at him. "How about being *more helpful* today then, instead of brave? We're all tired. You're strong. Find something to do to *help*. You can be brave another day."

"Okay. Can I dig holes, too?"

Tarra gave Puck a warm smile, swiping a forearm over her face to wipe at the dirt and sweat. She looked at his sling, still supporting his injured hand. "It takes two hands to shovel, Puck, and you just lost a finger. Olivia is not going to let you dig with that hand. Go ask her if you can help with something else."

Puck hurried around the corner of the house, Ozzie on his heels, to find Olivia and Gabby. They were on their knees under the living room window, tamping down the ground around a Prickly Pear Cactus with big leather gloves.

"Olivia, can I be helpful to you and Gabby today?" he asked, his eager face full of hope.

Gabby and Olivia exchanged curious glances.

Olivia shaded her eyes, and tilted her head, looking up at him. "No, Puck. I'm sorry, but these things hurt when they poke you. They can cause infection, too. You have to work on getting well again before you can help with stuff like this. What are you doing with that hose?"

Puck's lip poked out and he looked around for Grayson, his eyes squinted against the sun. "Taking it to the barn.

Graysie said to. Where's GrayMan? Can I help *him* with something?"

Olivia shook her head. "Grayson and Jake are cutting down trees. I don't want you near them. It's too dangerous for you, and them. They can't watch you and the blades, too."

She looked around the farm for *something* for Puck to do. There was a trail of brush, branches and deadfall that followed the tractor's trail from the woods to the road. She pointed at it. "See that stuff on the ground? That's the stuff that fell off the trees Elmer is hauling. All of it has to be gathered up. I don't know where they want it, so for now, just stack it up on the burn spot. If he doesn't need it for the camouflage project they're doing, we can burn it later. That'll help him to have it in one place."

Puck's eyes lit up. "I can burn it now! Where's a lighter?"

"No," Olivia told him firmly. "I don't want you playing with a lighter."

His shoulders drooped and he turned to walk away, kicking at a rock first.

He wasn't asking to *play* this time. He only wanted to help.

29

THE FARM

"HI, JENNY!" Puck threw the hose onto the ground outside the barn and hugged his donkey, showering her neck with kisses. "I've missed you, girl. I had to be *inside* doing chores today. I was being *helpful.*"

He ran his fingers under her new paracord harness. "Your necklace looks good on ya," he said, admiring his own handiwork.

He grabbed the handle of the yard wagon on wheels, and hurried through the yard, starting from the edge of the woods, all the way to the driveway, dragging the cart and loading it up with sticks, twigs, and brush, and bringing it the burn pile to dump several times. Jenny followed his every step, giving him encouragement, and Ozzie followed behind her, picking up any sticks that fell out of the wagon and running back and forth in front of Puck with them, begging for his attention.

Puck stopped and threw a stick for Ozzie a few times, until it felt like his hand had its own heartbeat, thumping and aching in rhythm with his real heartbeat.

In spite of his hurt, he was being *very* helpful, and hoped

GrayMan would come out of the woods to see him. He stole glances over his shoulder as he strutted, proud as a peacock, back and forth and back and forth.

Elmer passed him, giving him a nod, and it felt like a good nod, to Puck.

Olivia and Gabby smiled and waved, which felt nice too, but he really wanted to see that nod and smile from GrayMan.

He worked himself into a sweat and then he was done, with nothing left to carry. The pile was very big though and he wondered if GrayMan would move it. If GrayMan didn't need it, wouldn't it be *very helpful* for Puck to burn it for him?

He looked around for anything else he could do and saw the hose still needed put away. He scooped it up and carried it into the barn and stood still for a moment, his eyes squeezed close. It was darker in there, with the bright sunshine glaring down outside. He opened his eyes, taking a moment for them to adjust. He closed them again.

He swayed, and quickly opened them again, laughing at the funny feeling.

Jenny kicked up hay and dust as she followed Puck around the barn.

Where do I put this?

There were no hoses to be seen. Everything hanging on the walls looked like yard tools or barn-stuff. He didn't want to put it someplace wrong and GrayMan not be able to find it.

A door that led to a tack room was open and Puck poked his head in. The room was covered in cobwebs, but not dark like the rest of the barn. The tattered curtains were pulled back and the glass from the window was gone, letting the sun stream in. Someone had nailed a piece of plywood up, but it now hung from one nail, totally uncovering the window and letting in the elements.

Good thing it hasn't rained, Puck thought.

One shelf held three plastic five-gallon food-buckets. Grayson had moved them in there that morning before starting his project with Jake, just until he could deal with the roof leak in the container, not wanting to trust all the food they had to left to a possible bad seal on a bucket not holding up to a roof leak. He'd split it up, taking the chance on rain in one place, but the chance of rodents in the other, as the barn had seen its share of rats. He'd left some in the basement of the house, too.

Puck stepped in and dropped the garden hose on a low shelf and turned to leave, when he spied the new window-toy that Jake and Grayson had built.

He walked around it, hoping to take a peek, but it was covered in a heavy, dark blanket.

He thought about it a long time...it wasn't *his* toy...he knew he *shouldn't* use it.

But if he did, it could be helpful to GrayMan for him to at least move it outside next to the burn pile. Then if GrayMan was too hot and sweaty when he finished his project and wouldn't want to stand over a fire, maybe he'd let Puck do it.

Puck leaned around the door and peered out into the barn to see if it was still empty. There was no one there but him and Jenny, who stood just outside the tack room door, trying to shove a nosy nose into the doorway to see what he was doing.

"Hey, Jenny. *Shhh...*" He held his finger to his lips.

He reached out and lifted the blanket a teeny, tiny bit, using only two fingers, and peeked underneath.

The big frame rotated a bit, leaning toward him and making him jump.

Oh, how he wanted to play with this toy.

But it's not mine...

He heard a noise.

He let the blanket drop back down, quickly pulling his hand away, and hurried out the door into the main area of the barn, only to find Jenny having a face-off with Bacon Bit. The pig was in the stall that she'd claimed, against Jenny's wishes. Jenny didn't like sharing the barn, at least not with a pig.

Puck patted Jenny on her flank, and stood in front of Bacon Bit's stall. He stared at the fat little piglet, who stared right back with beady black eyes, poised to run. The men who'd brought her to the farm had scared her. She didn't trust anyone here so far and wouldn't allow anyone to love on her.

Puck had thought she was cute in her little tutu—what was left of it—until she'd stolen his ring.

GrayMan's ring.

He wondered where she'd hidden it. Maybe it was in that straw that she was rooting around in right now. *Do pigs hide things?*

Puck wrinkled his nose. There was a lot of poop in that hay, and he'd seen it in her mouth. Maybe she'd swallowed it?

If he found it, he'd be a hero.

He'd be a *helpful hero*.

He smiled wide, and stepped into the stall, causing Bacon Bit to squall in fear and run between his legs and out of the barn, nearly getting nipped by Jenny as she ran by.

Jenny followed Bacon Bit at a trot, leaving Puck to his task.

Just before he dug in for the treasure hunt, the blanket slid away from the Fresnel lens, pooling on the floor beneath it, unknowingly to Puck. As he dug through piles of straw and shit, the sun inched down a bit, filling the tack room with even more light.

30

THE FARM

THE BLAZING sun crept closer to the horizon, and Grayson and Jake were just about to finish up for the day. They'd felled close to two dozen trees, dragged them out of the woods, and loaded them onto the tractor, which Elmer had driven to the road and spent an ungodly amount of time haphazardly arranging just right—to look as though they weren't purposely arranged.

The driveway was now hidden from sight with a huge mound of crisscrossed trees topped with loose brush, and a passerby would see nothing but what appeared to be a rude dumping of logging and landscaping litter on a dead-end road already lined with forest.

They had a back way off the property to get Ruby out without being seen, too.

Grayson pulled off his gloves and blinked his eyes rapidly. "Do you see that, Jake?"

Jake gazed around him. "See what?"

"This." Grayson held his hand out, catching a few tiny gray flakes that floated slowly down from the blue sky, almost like snow.

"That's ash."

The men looked up, and saw a column of smoke rising.

They ran.

Flames crawled out the window of the tack room, swallowing air and growing ever taller, screaming like a bitch in the wind. The red paint peeled off in colorful, curly strips up and down the outside wall, and where the fiery fingers reached and grabbed for the old wood, it first lovingly kissed it—and then took a bite out of it, chewing it up in fierce, hot jaws.

Between the spaces in the old wood planks, the barn glittered with a hundred tiny flames.

They ran to the other side, finding smoke billowing out of the wide double doors, blocking their view inside.

Olivia, Gabby, Tina and Tarra came running, meeting them at the barn, everyone standing around in a panic, counting heads. Ozzie barked and crazily ran around their feet, nose to the air. A sudden breeze picked up, blowing a screen of smoke into their faces.

"Where's Graysie?" Grayson yelled, over the roar of the fire.

"In the house with the Littles," Olivia answered. "I checked on them just a few minutes ago. But where's Elmer?"

They all turned as one, seeing Elmer headed down the dirt road on the tractor. Grayson breathed a sigh of relief, as Elmer was known to wander in and out of the barn all day long.

"Get all the extra hoses together. Connect them and

bring me one end with a spray-nozzle, take the other end to Jake at the house! *Run*!" Grayson ordered.

Tina, Tarra and Gabby scattered, running to the garden and the wash tub area to do as he said and gather the hoses.

Grayson coughed, the smoke getting in his eyes. "Jake, you meet them there and connect the extra hoses to the outside faucet on the house. Since the house is already pressurized with the 12-volt RV pump, we'll get pressure through there, but you'll need to keep pumping the hand-pump to keep water moving into the tote. I'll fight the fire on this end, and trade out with you when your arm gets tired. *Hurry*!"

Jake turned to go, when their attention came back to the barn as Jenny ran up from behind them, clip-clopping her heels toward the dark, open double doors, passing Jake as he ran toward the pump. He skidded to a stop, turned and grabbed her by the braided paracord harness that Puck had adorned her neck with. "No, girl! You can't go in there!"

Jenny fought him, taking a nip at his shoulder and kicking in the air wildly.

"What the hell is wrong with this donkey?" Jake yelled. "You're supposed to run *away* from fire, you stubborn thing!" He tried with all his might to drag Jenny away, but she dug her heels in, pulling Jake toward the barn with her instead.

Grayson felt his blood drain. "Where's Puck?" he yelled to Olivia.

Olivia looked around, her eyes full of alarm. "I don't know. We saw him about a half hour ago..." she looked at Gabby, who had just returned dragging the first hose from the garden.

Gabby handed the end of the hose to Grayson, and pointed at the barn. "He was going in there to put away the garden hose from the basement! Maybe that's what's wrong with Jenny. Is Puck in there?"

Elmer skid to a stop on the tractor, and hurried down, almost falling. "What in tarnation? Is the boy in that mess?" he yelled. He snatched off his hat and pulled a bandana from his head, quickly tying it over his nose and mouth, and hurried toward the barn. "Cover your faces!"

Grayson stepped in front of him and held a hand out in the air. "No, Elmer! You're not going in there!"

"Well someone damn sure better go in there—and in a hurry—or I am," he yelled over the crackle of the fire. "That kid's gonna be a crispy critter if we don't move fast!"

The fire snapped loudly, startling everyone, but Grayson held firm. "We don't know that! Gabby, run to the house and look for Puck. Everyone else, hook up the hoses. Follow the plan… no use in someone getting hurt if he's not even in there. Now, go!" Grayson ordered.

Olivia stood still, her hand over her mouth. Her eyes watered and she waved the smoke from her face, squinting to try to see into the barn, while Jake tried to drag Jenny the other way—but she was set on going into the barn. He couldn't budge her.

Jenny honked and brayed, showing her teeth and wildly tossing her head. Kicking and dragging Jake an inch at a time, intent on meeting her blistering death, while he held on and tugged the other way.

"Olivia!" Grayson yelled. "Move *away*!" His head whipped around to Jake. "Jake, just let Jenny go!" Grayson threw his hands up into the air. "Get to the pump! Hurry before we lose the barn!"

Jake let go of Jenny, throwing his hands up in the air in frustration too, and the ass nearly tumbled backward onto her rump. She found her footing and rushed headfirst into the smoldering, swirling cloud, loudly braying and tossing her head.

31

THE FARM

GABBY RAN FROM THE HOUSE, screaming all the way. "He's not in here!"

Shivers went down Grayson's spine and he threw the hose down. "Dammit! *Puck!!*" he screamed. He grabbed his wallet and his gun and tossed them on the ground, and pulled a bandana out of his pocket, tying it around his face as he stomped toward the double doors, the smoke coming out in thick waves to welcome him. "I'm coming, kid!"

He really hadn't believed Puck was in there. Or maybe he didn't *want* to believe it. They weren't equipped for this... gone were the days of calling 911 and getting a fully-equipped fire truck, with men in fire-resistant suits and oxygen tanks who knew how to fight the fire.

They were on their own.

He'd denied to himself that Puck was in there, and now it might be too late.

A soot-covered nose broke through the cloud of smoke just as Grayson made it to the door, and with her came Puck stumbling along, being dragged by Jenny. He was barely able to stand upright, hanging onto her harness with one hand, and holding his shirt over his face with the other.

Grayson grabbed him and pulled him away from the barn, helping him to sit down against a tree, while the women slapped at the sparks on his clothes. "What happened, Puck? Are you okay?"

Puck coughed, trying to sputter out an answer, finally leaning over and vomiting. He swiped at his mouth and cleared his throat, coughing again.

Everyone gathered around him, Olivia dropping to her knees to check him for burns. She recoiled, wrinkling her nose. "What is that all over you, Puck?"

The boy was smeared with more than smoke and soot. His face, his shirt, his arms and his hands, held the shadow of smoke, but underneath, there was something more.

"Mama Dee always said if there was a fire, to stop, drop and roll. I was in Bacon Bit's stall when I saw it." He held up his good hand and Olivia cringed. It was covered in smelly, brown pig shit. "And look, GrayMan. I got your..." *cough, cough...* "ring back."

Later that day, it was determined the fire was started by the Fresnel lens. They lost that, and all the food preps that had been moved into the tack room. The remains of the long-term food stored in plastic buckets were nothing more than puddles. The food that had been inside was a bit overcooked.

The tack room was a total loss, but the rest of the barn was mostly intact. At least it hadn't been razed to the ground.

That didn't lesson Grayson's anger, especially when the boy could only answer his questions with a, 'I just wanted to be a hero, GrayMan,' and when he'd admitted to digging through pile after pile of pig shit just to find his ring, which made Grayson feel even worse in the face of his anger.

The facts were, they were now shorter on food—again—and could have lost Puck, Jenny and even Bacon Bit, too, whom still had yet to reappear.

Just the thought of losing all that bacon nearly made Grayson lose his mind.

He ranted and raved at the boy about his carelessness, until Olivia made him stop, assuring him that his point was made, and Puck had tearfully slithered off to the basement for the night, after tying Jenny to a tree. The barn needed a good airing out before she slept in there again.

Jenny received an extra special supper that night, picked fresh from the garden, and Olivia spoke kindly to her, thanking her for saving the boy.

The next morning, Grayson's voice thundered through the house. "Where's Puck? Anyone seen him?"

His question was met with shrugs. No one knew.

He'd met the sun early, the dawn-sky revealing the nights horrors. But the thing that was bothering him the most was Puck's need to be a hero. He'd have to shake that notion out of the boy, or no one would be safe from his quests.

The front door opened and Jake stepped in. "Grayson, what did you do with that map I made to the camp? We gonna get started that way to check on Tucker and everyone?"

"I don't have it."

"You were driving when I put it in the glove box of my truck."

Grayson held his hands up. "I know; I remember. But I haven't touched it."

"It's gone."

Grayson stomped down the hallway to Graysie's room, finding Briar and Brody alone in her bed, their blonde heads snuggled up to each other fast asleep.

He came back to the living room. "Where's Graysie?"

Olivia stood up. "She's not in there? Maybe she's outside?"

"No, I've been all over the farm. She's not out there. Jenny's gone, too."

Concern painted their faces. Graysie wasn't an early riser, unless forced. She was still a teenage girl and would rather sleep than do most anything.

Olivia grabbed her shoes and sat down, shoving her feet into them as fast as she could. "Where do you think they are?"

Grayson shook his head. "I'd imagine Puck is off to that damn camp *to be a hero*...and Graysie went to save his ass. And by that, I *don't* mean Jenny."

32

CAMP

GRAYSON, Jake and Elmer snuck through the woods, having left Ruby parked and hidden a few miles away. They had no idea what they were walking into, and didn't want to risk their only means of transportation.

Grayson army-crawled on his belly, dragging his rifle with him, the last few feet before the edge of the woods. Jake was right beside him, and Elmer on his left with his shotty, painfully trying to keep up with the two younger men, his old knees and elbows protesting.

They eyeballed the camp. The concertina wire on the top of the fence promised a slow death, but the guard in the tower pointing an AR15 guaranteed to make it quicker.

"What do you make of it?" Elmer grumbled in a low voice. "If it's supposed to help people, what's with the barbed wire and the guard tower? That guard don't look none too friendly."

The kids' camp had definitely been converted...to something. It didn't look like any kid's camp Grayson had ever seen. The log cabins made sense, but the fence, wire and guards roving around said it was something more than what it had been. Seemed like Nick was right.

Grayson harrumphed. "FEMA, my ass..." he mumbled.

A guard dressed in camo walked by the inside of the fence, and was met with a skinny, haggard man approaching him. The man's clothes were filthy, and his cheeks were hollowed.

Grayson held a hand up. "*Shhh*... let's see if we can hear them," he whispered.

They tucked their heads down and listened.

The haggard man carried a knapsack. Just a shirt, tied up around a bundle, it appeared. He was motioning toward the gate, and soon his motions became frantic. They couldn't hear their exact words, but they could hear a pleading tone, met with an abrasive, forceful one. The guard shoved the man away with the butt of his rifle, and yelled forcefully, "You're not going anywhere!"

"That answers that," Grayson whispered. He motioned for them to back up, when a group of four sturdy men walked by the gate, wearing jeans with leather vests, no shirts underneath. All four carried rifles in meaty, muscular arms, painted heavily in ink, including the word, 'TWO' prominently displayed and framed in tribal markings.

"Wait," Grayson whispered, pointing at the men. "Is that—?"

Jake cringed.

Three of the men were unfamiliar, but the fourth rang his bell.

It was *Smalls*—the man he'd let walk away from the farm after they'd buried his buddies.

Grayson quietly waved them back and they belly-crawled the way they'd come, standing up when they were a safe distance away.

He swallowed hard and fixed Jake with a hard stare.

Elmer looked back and forth at the two of them, then realization dawning, he snatched his hat off, and slapped his leg with it. "You mean to tell me that's one of the men that killed my Edith? The men that branded my bride like a damn animal?"

Jake rubbed his hand over his face. "I'm sorry, Elmer. Yeah, that's him. I should've listened to Grayson...we shouldn't have let him go."

Grayson took a deep breath and exhaled. He cuffed Jake on the arm, while Elmer marched off to get his thoughts together, and calm down. "No, you did what you thought was right. I'm as surprised as you, really. Can't believe that fucker survived the gunshot wound and got this far on foot. If there's four of them, and one in the tower, there's probably more armed men, too."

He scratched his beard. "Looks like we're going to need some help. You think Gabby can call in the Calvary again?"

Puck woke up in a daze, rubbing his noggin with his hurt hand. The air was stifling and he had a searing pain in his head. His temples pounded with a rhythm that matched his hand. He gasped and pulled it away to look. *It hurt.* Worse than ever. The bandage was bloody and very dirty. His sling was gone, too, so he hadn't been keeping his arm up like he was supposed to.

Olivia was gonna fuss at him.

He looked around, his eyes still blurry, further confusing him as to where he was, and nearly jumped in surprise to find a dog on either side of him, napping in the sweltering heat.

"Hoss! Daisy!" he exclaimed happily. "I found you!" The dogs lifted their heads, with little to no energy. Their fur was matted with blood and they looked thinner than they had just a few days ago. Puck took turns petting and smoothing their hair with his good hand, while he held his injured hand tightly against his chest.

His jail was a ten by ten dog kennel, the top covered with reinforced barbed wire. It was concreted into the ground. With no shade, the sun beat down on top of the him and the dogs. There was no water to be seen. He was sitting up, leaned against the far side of the gate, which was locked with a heavy chain and padlock.

A heap of dirty blankets on the far side of the kennel caught his eye.

Is that moving?

Soon, a low growl filled the air and Hoss and Daisy struggled to their feet, stepping in front of Puck in a territorial stance, and returning the growl in unison.

The heap of blankets moved again and a big dog emerged. It wasn't blankets after all; it was a stout Pit Bull-mix dog, with one torn ear. His oversized-face was covered with scratches, old and new, and with scabs, and his boxy body crisscrossed in scars. The dog shakily rose to his feet and lowered his head. Saliva ran out of both sides of his mouth as he pulled his lips back in a snarl.

The smell of bad meat filled Puck's nose and as the dog limped forward a few steps, he saw the cause of it. The dog's leg was severely infected.

Tucker's two American Bulldogs met the Pit's approach with two slow steps of their own, lowering their heads, their hackles rising. Three growls filled the air in disharmony, raising Puck's own hair on the back of his neck. He held his breath, afraid to make a single move.

The Pit turned and heavily lay down, seemingly not interested in a fight at the moment. He growled once more for good measure as he melted back onto the concrete slab, and Puck exhaled in relief.

Slowly, he remembered what had happened, and how he'd got to this place.

He trembled at the flood of memories.

Following Jake's map had been easy. Like he'd said, it was a straight shot. He just wanted to check to see if Tucker's dogs were here, and help get them back. He didn't know the soldier would *promise* to let him in to take a look, but then lie and take his gun, and want him to *stay*.

The man in camo didn't let him look for Tucker's dogs after all.

Mama Dee said never to argue with adults, but GrayMan said when a man doesn't keep his word, he should be called out on it. When Puck did that, the man got mean, so he tried to leave. But he may have back-talked just a little bit too much.

The man *still* wouldn't open the gate, and Puck wanted to go home, so he'd tried to climb the fence. The mean man pulled him down, and they fought.

Puck was winning, but soon there were more soldiers, and they didn't fight fair. They knocked him down to the ground with their big guns.

He wished he'd not let them have *his* gun.

And then Jenny had shown up...with Graysie right behind her.

In seconds, they had guns trained on Graysie and told her to drop her pistol she was aiming at them. They promised they'd shoot him, and then her in the time it took her to shoot one of them.

Graysie had dropped her gun, but they were still going to *shoot* Jenny right through the gate! Just for fun.

He couldn't let that happen.

He'd jumped up and shoved the gun, just before it'd went off, and a round had slammed into one of the men, instead.

Puck's heart beat faster, thinking of the way the man had crumpled to the ground, hugging his gut, with blood seeping out around his fingers. It hadn't looked real. It was like one of his video games.

He was going to be in so much trouble.

And then the last thing he remembered was a blinding flash.

Puck slapped at a swarm of mosquitos. He adjusted his weight on the hard concrete, and craned his stiff neck, looking around, wondering where Jenny and Graysie were now, and if Graysie would make the mean men let him go.

An hour Earlier:

Graysie fought like a wildcat, trying to get onto the other side of the fence, her gun in the dirt at her feet. She hadn't had a choice. They were going to put a bullet in him, if she didn't surrender it.

Her red curls bounced as she shook the wire with both hands. "Get off of him! Leave him alone," she screamed at the men who'd beat Puck down to the ground. "Let me in!"

Puck lay unconscious on the ground, not far from another man who lay bleeding with his finger stuck in the hole that had punctured through his gut. The man's eyes were wide and panicked and his brow wrinkled in concentration. He lay very still, blinking rapidly. He didn't look more than twenty years old, just a few years older than Graysie herself.

The other three men Puck had fought with gave Graysie a wide smile, ignoring their friend in a bloody heap laying at their feet, waiting for help or death. One of them worked quick to open the lock. "Sure. Everybody welcome here. You know this boy?" he asked through the fence, and then opened the gate wide, waving his arm in the air, welcoming her in. "After you..."

Graysie, confused by his welcome after such a vicious attack on Puck, stuttered, "Yyy-es. He's my...er...brother," she lied. "And that's our donkey. Don't hurt her. Just let me take my brother home—and his donkey."

Another guard approached Jenny with a gleam in his eye and his arms spread wide. The donkey blew at him.

Graysie tried to shoo her away. "Run, Jenny!"

But Jenny didn't shy away. She twitched her long ears and blew another loud and arrogant breath at the man, as though in contempt, and proudly hurried in straight to Puck, nudging his leg, while the men stood around smiling at their windfall of good luck, even in spite of one of their own lying near death in the dirt.

The guard shut the gate and locked it quickly behind them.

Graysie fell to the ground next to Puck, breathing hard and feeling for a pulse. Her ears were ringing. "Puck, you okay?"

Puck didn't answer.

"Your big brother just shot the boss' nephew."

"No, he didn't. You did! I saw what happened." She found a strong pulse and breathed a sigh of relief. "And he's my *little* brother. I'm older," she jabbed back at the man. "Puck, wake up..."

"Little brother is a big 'un," the guard said and laughed. "Bigger they are, harder they fall." He bumped her leg with his boot, and looked outside the gate, giving the gravel road a long look. He smiled wolfishly. "Where's the rest of your family, Little Red Riding Hood?"

The other two men laughed.

Graysie kept her eyes on Puck, waving a fly away from his face, and bristled at the remark. She looked around, stalling for time. The camp was dusty and quiet, with a few people shuffling around in the distance. Far off to one side, she could see a garden, with a few dozen people peppered throughout it, bent over under the scorching sun working it; some were hoeing, and some were squatting...either weeding or picking, she couldn't be sure.

At a larger log-cabin style building, located in the middle of the camp, was a very long line of people, mostly women, looking forlorn and haggard, *or* frazzled and panicked. In unkempt clothes, mostly shorts and tank-tops, their backs were knobby and hunched over, and their shoulders protruded out like pointy blades, as they stood with their heads down under the watchful glare of another angry-looking man standing on the porch, a rifle slung over his shoulder.

Many of the women—a huge majority who looked no older than early to mid-twenties, if that—had bedraggled, grubby children beside them, clinging tightly to their hands. Their faces were dirty, their hair greasy and they were nearly in rags.

There was no running, or playing.

No smiles or happy faces, as they clung desperately to their mother's hands.

Graysie squinted at the line of women, noticing several of them bore the number "2" on their arms in an angry, red welt.

She swallowed hard, choked by fear, and numbed by her terror.

Elmer had told them what happened to Edith...who was also branded with the 2.

She looked down at Puck, and swatted another fly away from his innocent, sleeping face. The realization that they were now *locked into* this sad, desolate, and terrible place hit her like a bucket of water in the face. Puck was in terrible trouble, and she and Jenny with him.

She wanted to leave this place—immediately.

Graysie had refused to answer any questions on her family's whereabouts, not willing to risk anyone going after her kin or their supplies. In tears, she was half-dragged away from Puck, the guards assuring her they'd 'take care of him.' They took her down a path to a row of four very small cabins, where the tattooed men argued over her as though she were a side of beef, until one who obviously pulled rank arrived, quieting the other men with only his presence.

He was a giant of a man, but the patch on his vest read, 'Smalls.'

Graysie swallowed down her fear. This was the same animal that had been to the farm. He was the lone survivor that Olivia had patched up. Puck had killed his buddies. When he saw Puck, it was *really* going to be over. She ducked her head, hoping he didn't recognize her.

Smalls stepped up to her, putting a finger on her chin, lifting her face.

She tossed her head, throwing her red curls over her shoulder and removing his finger. She stared at him defiantly, her green eyes narrowing. She wouldn't show fear to him; she knew better than that. These types of men thrived on it.

Neither of the two blinked. Finally, he pointed to her new home with a firm nod. "Get in there," he said, his voice a low rumble.

The other three men grumbled, and one stepped up. "Why is it you always get the youngest, prettiest ones, Smalls?"

Smalls turned, finding the smaller man in his space. He closed the gap with one step, bumping up against his chest, and stared down at the man, fire in his eyes. "You want to challenge me for her? Say the word..." he snarled.

The man quickly shook his head and backed off. "No," he was quick to answer.

Smalls turned back, just as Graysie was about to make a run for it. He snatched her by the back of the shirt and lifted her onto the top step in one quick movement, and smacked her ass. She could feel his hot breath on her neck.

She grimaced and hurried forward two steps, eager to put space between them. It was a basic building, no more than something people put in their back yards for lawn equipment storage, with a rough plywood floor and two windows. It had a small shaded porch outside, and the door was painted in red spray paint with a huge number two, and hung wide open, showing an even more dismal inside.

She hesitated, receiving a not too gentle shove, and stumbled in. Six bunks displayed a ratty collection of bedding, and a few pillows. There was one single-bed inside, made up neat and tidy with sheets and a somewhat nice blanket, which she assumed were his. There were several foot-lockers, but only one end table, cluttered with a scattering of miscellaneous belongings.

The bunks were empty, with the exception of one. An older Hispanic woman, pretty for her years, lay stretched out on a bottom bed. She hurried to her feet in a panic at their entrance.

She pushed her long, straight black and silver hair out of her eyes. "Sorry, Smalls. I only laid down for a minute," she explained. "I was just about to get up and check on the girls."

Smalls cut her a glance, and waved her back to her bunk. "Teach her the ropes," he said, gesturing at Graysie with his thumb, and walked out the door.

The woman exhaled in relief.

33

CAMP

UPON SMALL'S QUICK EXIT, Graysie ran to one of the windows, looking out over the camp. All she could see were more cabins and trees. No fence though. Maybe she could find Puck and escape.

"Give it up. You can't get out of here," the woman told her. She held out her hand. "I'm Silva. I'm sort of the Cabin Mom here."

Graysie turned and studied the woman. She was only a few years older than her stepmom, Olivia. Silva had tired eyes, crinkled at the corners, and a very kind face. She shook her hand. "What are you doing here?"

Silva shrugged. "Came with my two daughters. Thought this was a Fema camp; here to help us. It's not exactly that... not anymore."

"What is it?"

"It's a camp, but Fema left weeks ago. Run off by the guy in charge, Cutter, the head of a rogue militia. He partnered up with this biker gang and they ran off what little bit of government was here. This is not a good place. What's your name?"

"Graysie."

"You have family?"

"Yeah, but they're not here. I mean, other than my brother," she lied again. "He's not right in the head. Our dad doesn't know we came. He got in trouble yesterday and took off, so I followed him to make sure he was okay. Didn't know he was walking right into this place."

"Well, you're both stuck here now, so count your blessings you ended up in this cabin. The rest are worse. Much worse. I'll show you. But first, are you hungry?"

Graysie nodded. She hadn't eaten since the day before.

Silva stuck her arm under her pillow, coming out with a bright red tomato and a cucumber. She held them both out to Graysie. "Your choice."

Graysie looked at her in confusion.

"Trust me, girl. This is a treat compared to what you'll be eating here. May as well get used to it."

Graysie took the tomato, biting into it with a grimace, as the juice leaked out and down her chin. She swiped at it. "Thank you. Can you take me to find my brother? And his donkey..."

Silva looked at her in surprise.

"Don't ask...it's a long story."

"I have no idea where your brother's at, but if there's a donkey, I think I might know where you'll find it."

Silva rolled a hand in the air, and her head whipped around, looking out the door and both windows. "Hurry and eat that. You can't take it with us. We'll get in trouble for having it."

They began her tour at the next cabin, where they stood just outside the open window watching in horror—at least Graysie did... it seemed Silva wasn't at all surprised by what they saw.

One of the bikers—his patch printed with his name: Nat —was sitting on his bed with a young woman who was beautiful, in spite of her ragged clothes and dirty face. He slid his hand down her arm and she cringed in revulsion.

Angry, he reached into a coffee can and came up with a tiny, pink, hairless mouse by the tail. It wiggled and squirmed furiously and the woman cringed away from it, leaning into two terrified children who huddled behind her in fright, fresh tearstains on their faces.

"Please," she begged.

"Would you rather..." the biker taunted. "Eat this wee little mouse, sleep with me, *or* let your little crumbsnatchers go hungry another day..."

Graysie recoiled at his words and looked at Silva in shock.

She whispered to Graysie. "It's a little fucked up game they play. That woman and her kids haven't eaten in two days. This piece of shit wants to bed her, but Cutter will have his ass unless she agrees to it first. We have a No Rape Policy here. It gets broken sometimes, but these guys will try to break the girls first and do it the easy way—easy for them, anyway—rather than invoke Cutter or Smalls' wrath."

"Cutter?"

"Yeah, he's the boss."

"I've seen him. He came to my aunt and uncle's neighborhood, offering sanctuary here."

"Yeah, he's the head recruiter. Let me guess...did someone steal their food first? Or did they have a fire?"

"Their food was stolen. But what does he want with these people if he's already getting the guns and food? Why keep more mouths to feed?"

"Entertainment for one." Silva gestured at the window and Graysie's eyes returned just in time to see the woman obediently open her mouth, like a baby bird, leaning her head back with her eyes clenched tightly closed, but not tight enough to keep the tears from streaming out the edges. She held one of her children's hands in each of her own. She shook violently.

The man held the frightened mouse over her open mouth, where it fought against the dark hole it hovered over, it's tiny hands and feet grabbing hold of the sides of her mouth and spreading itself out like a big 'X.'

The man laughed and poked it in with his fat, stubby finger, and then clamped the woman's jaw shut with a rough grip. "Chew it," he demanded hatefully.

The woman heaved, sobbing through a mouthful and chewing rapidly, trying to kill the squirming rodent with her teeth. Graysie heaved along with her, covering her own mouth with her hand. Silva pulled her away before they caught his attention.

They hurried past the rest of the cabins, coming to a huge planted field on one side, and a work area on the other. Silva waved a hand around her. "Here's the other reason."

Graysie turned in a circle, looking all around her. Here was another guard tower, looking over a line of heavy equipment parked inside a locked fence on one side. A farm tractor with front-end loader, a Bobcat skid steer, and the military trucks that Graysie had seen come into Tullymore were lined up.

"Where do they get the gas to run all that stuff?"

Silva shrugged. "I don't know, but they have plenty. They keep it in tanks right behind the trucks. You can't see them from here. I'm sure they *took* it just like everything else," she whispered the last part, glancing up at the guard.

The guard tower also overlooked the field and work area.

A handful of men were chopping and splitting wood off to one side, throwing it into a truck-sized pile, with a guard in green fatigues standing over them, his rifle hanging from a sling at his waist. In the field, dozens more worked silently under watchful eyes. They moved slowly, obviously tired and hot, from the looks of their soaked and soiled clothing.

"They need people to work so they can eat and have clean clothes. And other amenities. They take the teenage boys out on scavenger hunts, sending them into places first in case someone gets hurt. The men are also forced to work outside the camp as often as not, lately. But we don't know what they're doing. When they come back—and they always do because they only take the men who have family here—they won't talk for days. No one but the militia and the bikers know what's going on outside these gates."

In another area, woman and teenage girls worked over hot, boiling cauldrons, stirring laundry with wooden oars, while some hung it to dry on a long clothes line.

"See those cages over there?" Silva pointed to two large iron cages that sat near the guard towers, directly in the sun. "Those are used to scare people. That's our 'jail.' So far, I haven't seen them used for anything but separating stray dogs before they fight them."

"Dogs?"

Silva nodded. "Big and little. The little ones are used as bait to train the bigger ones. Most that come here have never fought before. They don't feed them for days, then hang one of the little dogs from a tree, and make it bleed. The bigger dogs are starving by then, and fight over it."

Graysie shuddered, thinking of Hoss and Daisy and wondering if they were here.

She followed Silva and walked past the two work areas and stopped at a lean-to shack that was set off from the beaten path. The air around the shack was heavy with a tangy, coppery smell that turned Graysie's stomach. Heavy tarps were hung from the porch roof, mostly blocking Graysie's view inside, with the exception of two huge, bloody hooks that were mounted to the porch walls. From one hung a furry rabbit, and from the other, a handful of squirrels, all tied together by their tails.

On the wooden plank floor were huge spots of blood, looking all the world like left-over spills of red paint, and a pile of assorted vacated animal skins, waiting to be processed. Graysie stared at the top of the pile, into the empty hulls of a cat's eyes staring back at her. Its fur was a striped orange. A regular house-cat.

Near a dilapidated rocking chair was a metal bucket, filled to the rim with rusty, bloody, metal tools.

Outside the lean-to, a deer hung from a tall tree, a jagged line cut into its belly and its guts dropping in a steaming pile onto the ground.

A greasy-looking, chubby man in overalls working in front of the deer turned around, wiping his knife on an already-bloody apron. He shot a look to the guard in the tower, gave him a quick suggestive wink, and leered at Graysie with a broken line of teeth, the gaping holes even more sinister than the rotten teeth he did still possess.

He licked his lips.

Graysie shivered in spite of the heat, and Silva put her arm around her protectively. "This one is Smalls," she said, her chin stuck out. "Hands off."

Silva led her away. In a whisper, she said, "If there's a donkey in the camp, it's probably in there somewhere." She pointed with her chin to the horrific lean-to as they passed it, nearly bringing Graysie to her knees.

34

THE FARM

GRAYSON PACED THE FLOOR, waiting on Jake and Gabby to return.

They'd left hours earlier, with plans to make contact with Gabby's MAG group. It was the mutual assistance group of prepper friends she'd met on the internet, the same group that had saved their bacon once before, in the grocery store.

He'd have preferred to have gone with Jake and Gabby, but had sent Tina and Tarra instead, choosing to stay home and guard the farm with Elmer, while trying to calm Olivia and Ozzie down.

Both were nearly frantic.

He was proud of Olivia for not falling apart—yet—after hearing their news of the camp, and Smalls, the biker from the TWO gang. It helped that she had the Littles: Briar and Brody, in her shadow, watching and listening to every word. She didn't want to scare the children with her own tears.

In typical Olivia-style, she was a whirlwind of cooking and cleaning, constantly checking the window for signs of her sister, and the company she might bring, her face filled with worry.

Hours later, Gabby arrived with a hope and a prayer.

She'd found the MAG group's bug-out location. But all were gone, other than Pete. When she relayed the story to Pete, and asked for their help, he made plans to meet down the road from the camp the day after next, after the rest of his group was due to return from a scavenging trip in town.

Grayson had cursed their luck and slammed his fist into a wall, not wanting to wait. But he was no idiot. There was no way his small group could go up against so many guns alone, and they might only have one chance. He hoped both his daughter and Puck could hold on...

35

CAMP

LATE THE NEXT MORNING, Cutter stood outside the dog pen, his eyes narrowed at Puck, and his hand hovering over his sidearm. His fingers danced in anticipation. "How'd you do that, boy?"

When Puck saw Cutter coming, he knew the man was mad. He walked with angry steps and he had a scary face, and it wasn't just the scar that scared him. It was his eyes.

He'd scurried to the farthest corner of the pen, and put his back against the wire and his butt on the concrete, trying to make himself small. The three dogs followed and turned, standing in formation between him and the gate where Cutter stood. The canines were shoulder to shoulder; the Pit taking center position.

All three dogs bared their teeth at the man, daring him to come in.

"Do what?" Puck asked in confusion.

"That Pit right there...that's *my* dog. He don't take kindly to strangers, he doesn't get along with other dogs, and he *definitely* doesn't growl at *me*. He knows I'll kick his fucking teeth in. What'd you do to him?" Cutter demanded.

"Mister, if this is your dog, you haven't been very nice to him. He's all messed up."

Cutter sneered at him, his scar wrinkling in distaste and his lips curled.

Puck cringed backward, pressing his back against the wire, and willed himself to be brave. "I think you've been mean to this here dog, mister. And that's not very nice," he mumbled.

"What are you, a retard?"

Puck gasped. "Mama Dee doesn't allow *anyone* to call me that, sir. That's not very nice either. You have bad manners."

Cutter shook his head in disbelief.

Earlier in the day, someone had brought food and water to the dogs and Puck. He'd saved his to trade, waiting for another kid to walk by. There'd been plenty of them all morning passing through in a hurry, stealing fearful glances at both him and the Pit. The next that came by was more than happy to take his trade; his food for a bottle of the clear medicine in a brown bottle that made bubbles when Mama Dee poured it on his scratches, and some clean bandages.

It'd taken over an hour, but the kid had come through, greedily trading the tin plate of cold scrambled eggs—mostly runny anyway—and burnt, curled Spam for exactly what Puck had asked for.

He'd let the dogs drink their fill of the water, and then slowly made his way toward the Pit with the water that was left over and the supplies, scooting on his bottom and looking a different direction. He's sang a quiet song under his breath, ignoring the dog. It had taken a long time to get close enough, an inch at a time, but Puck eventually coaxed the dog into letting him into his space. Then he'd cleaned the bad leg and bandaged it up.

After that, he'd ran his fingers gently over the Pit, and

sang to him some more, eventually working up to rubbing his sore muscles and earning a loyal friend. Hoss and Daisy had cautiously crept closer and closer until they saw the Pit accepted them as well. They finished the job by cleaning the older dog's scratches on his face with their tongues while he lounged back and ate up the unfamiliar attention and companionship.

They were a pack now...and the pack had turned on Cutter.

Puck put a protective hand on the Pit, and scratched his back, cooing to him in baby-talk. Cutter spit on the ground and furiously grabbed the padlock, digging in his pocket for the key, when Smalls walked up.

"What're you gonna do to that kid?" he asked.

Cutter looked over his shoulder at the bigger man, and then back to the lock. "Not sure yet. My nephew died last night, so this kid owes me, and it's a debt that can only be paid in blood."

Now Puck shook in fear. He hadn't meant to shoot that man. He was just trying to stop them from shooting Jenny. He was sorry that he died.

Cutter fumbled with the key, almost getting it in, when Smalls moved his hand, shoving the key away from the lock. "I want this kid."

Cutter turned around and scoffed. "That's weird, even for you, Smalls. But no can-do. He's mine."

"I'm not asking. I'm *telling* you," Smalls growled, standing up to his full height, which was well over four inches taller than the smaller man.

The two men circled each other like mad bulls, one in fatigues, and one in jeans and a leather vest. Both men covered in ink and meaner than two snakes.

"You can't have them all, Smalls. You already got the girl."

"Your men have the donkey."

Puck stood up. "That's *my* donkey! That's Jenny. Where is she?" He ran to the gate, his eyes wide, his fear for himself gone now. "Is Jenny okay?"

Cutter laughed. "Jenny? Damn boy, you are a retard. Couldn't think of anything more unique than that? I assure you, Jenny is good. Or she will be when the cook gets done with her."

Puck looked at him in confusion.

"Leave the kid alone," Smalls demanded. "Don't tell him that shit, and don't use that word, either."

"What the fuck, man? You seriously got a hard-on for this kid, or what?"

"1980 called. They want that word back. And you and I agreed there'd be no unusual cruelty here. That was the deal."

Cutter scoffed again. "Unusual cruelty? That mule is meat. It'd be cruel not sharing it with the people we have here."

Puck shook the fence. "She's not a mule! And I *will* share! Jenny has enough love for everybody!"

Cutter shook his head at Puck, and laughed. "This kid is a moron."

Smalls stepped in front of the gate. "The people here would eat fine if your men would give them some of that food they've been hoarding for themselves. You don't need to mess with the donkey."

Cutter backed up a step. "*Your* men are eating pretty good too. So are the women they've claimed for themselves, I hear."

"I say good to that. Everybody deserves to eat. We've got

plenty," Smalls answered with a shrug. "Now, unlock the gate. I'm taking this boy back to my cabin."

"No, you're not."

"I *am*," Smalls roared.

A small crowd had gathered, eager to see the two head honchos of the camp go at it. Cutter and Smalls realized their mistake and both stood down. Cutter yelled at the crowd, "Get back to work, or no food rations today."

They scattered.

Smalls still stood in front of the gate, an unmovable mountain.

Cutter sighed. "Look, Smalls...let's not split hairs here. How about come to my office and we'll sort this out."

"The boy safe here?"

"For now. But know this... there will be payback for my nephew, and it can only be blood. But we can work something out."

Smalls paused, glaring at him. "You lead," he finally answered.

Puck watched the men stomp off to decide his fate, and he sunk down to the concrete, one hand still grasping the fence, worry for Jenny squeezing his heart.

36

CAMP

Two long sleepless nights passed, with Graysie tucked into the corner of a top bunk, uncomfortably sweating, and quietly swatting at mosquitos all night. She'd been fed only twice, both times a plate of rice and beans, the two days prior, and her constant requests to see Puck had finally raised the ire of Smalls, who until then hadn't so much as looked her way.

He'd screamed at her to shut up, and sent her to bed.

She'd spent yesterday on her new work assignment, picking June bugs off row after row of tomato vines. She reeked with their putrid smell, and she repeatedly cursed the southern bug that sprayed the toxic-smelling fumes to warn off its enemies. She must've picked a thousand, dropping them into a tiny hole in a screen into a bucket...and her legs ached from the constant squats, but her job was better than some she'd seen.

The TWO gang made sure their girls were assigned the best jobs, as most of them didn't want the women too tired when they returned to their bunks at night. Silva said in the other cabins, the women were treated like house-slaves, made to wash and groom the bikers—and other things—as ordered. When Graysie asked what Smalls required of *his* girls, Silva hushed her, sending Graysie a quiet nod toward one of the girls at the bunk across the room.

Silva tapped her ear, and then made the universal sign for 'talks too much' with her hand, and she hadn't been given a private moment since with the Cabin Mom to ask all the questions on her troubled mind.

But it wasn't a worry the first two nights, as Smalls came to bed long after they did, not purposely waking anyone as he came in. Silva would jump up to do his bidding, and he'd wave her back down again, sending her back to bed in relief.

Graysie didn't let that soothe her qualms. She didn't trust him and slept with one eye open, if she slept at all. When she felt herself nod off, she'd pinch the underside of her arm as hard as she could. At this point, she was nearly catatonic with exhaustion and the need for sleep.

Now she lay quietly watching the sun fill the dismal cabin, and thought of home while listening to Smalls snore. The past few hours had been quiet. Before that, she'd listened to several of her cabin-mates quietly weeping off and on. Throughout the night, she'd watched Silva, creeping by moonlight, from one bunk to another, offering comfort and sometimes a few nibbles of food to the four other girls there with them—all of who were Graysie's age, including two that were Silva's own daughters.

Graysie wondered what terrible things Smalls had inflicted upon these women and when it would be her turn. Her eyes and mind were in constant motion trying to figure out how to get her hands on a weapon, or how to *make* one. So far, the only weapons she'd seen—other than the pistol Smalls kept under his pillow when he slept—were the ones the guards or the bikers carried with them, or the rifle that she watched Smalls put in a footlocker before he laid down to sleep.

Even a knife or fork were out of the question, as they were made to eat with plastic sporks. Graysie bit her lip wondering if she could grab his pistol from beneath his pillow before waking him. It would be a huge risk... but one she might be willing to take to get Puck and go home. She made her mind up. If Smalls called her to his bed, she wouldn't give in without a fight. She'd learned long ago to fight like a man...and she would make a grab for that gun and do her daddy proud.

The room was roused with the beep of Small's watch, and Graysie watched as the girls sat up, waiting patiently for Smalls to rise first, and dress in the small space. Silva assisted him, handing his socks and boots to him one at a time, then standing back while he retrieved his gun belt and pistol from under his pillow and buckled it on, and then unlocked the foot locker and retrieved his rifle on a sling.

He slung it over his shoulder and then spoke to the women. "There's a gathering down at the amphitheater just before breakfast. Everyone needs to be there. Y'all sit together and behave. Save me a spot, Silva."

Silva nodded respectfully.

He looked at Graysie. "You... are expected at Cutter's office this morning. You go straight there. Silva, take her there now and then come back here. I have a project for y'all."

Silva nodded again.

Smalls opened the door and pulled in a heavy roll of plastic sheeting and a roll of silver duct tape that he must've brought late the night before. "You've got one hour before you need to walk down to the amphitheater, so don't dally around. Be quick about this. I want it done before you go."

He held up the plastic. "Use this plastic to seal the cabin. First, cover these two windows. Then pull all the bunks out and put it over *every* wall. I don't want to see one tiny crack that's not covered. Just tape it at the ceiling and let it drape all the way to the floor, all the way around. Tape it down. On the door, hang two pieces. One over the inside of the door, and then attach one over the outside of the door. If you have any left, cover the floor."

Silva risked a feeble joke. "Going all Dexter on us, Smalls?" she asked nervously.

One of her daughters meekly spoke up. "It'll get blistering hot in here if we do that, Smalls...we need some air passing through."

Smalls slowly blinked his eyes twice at the women and continued. "Just do what I say. Line the pieces up close so you can tape them together too, other than the last one. We'll need to get in and out the door. On the porch, you'll find water, and a box with some food and other things in it. Pull it inside, but do *not* eat the food or drink the water. Don't even open the box yet. If something happens, you all run back here as fast as you can. Shut the door behind you. I'll be here soon after."

"Something like what?" Silva asked. "And when is this happening?"

"I don't know. It could be today, tomorrow, next week or next month...or maybe never," he said mysteriously. "But you'll know what I'm talking about when and if it does happen, and I want to be prepared for it. So just do what I tell you to do. If it does happen, and if I don't make it back here, open the box. You'll know then what to do with what's inside. If you open it before then, I'll know. And I'll be *very* angry."

He turned to leave, pausing at the door and throwing one last look at Graysie from over his shoulder. He sighed heavily and blew his breath out his nose, then left with regret in his eyes.

37

CAMP

In perfect timing with the gloomy mood, the summer storm they'd all been praying for finally arrived, breaking through the skies, giving an ominous backdrop to the amphitheater.

This place was off away from the main camp, through a trail in the woods and was heavily guarded because if someone could manage to swim to the other side, there was no fence there. Only the most trusted of the refugees were allowed at the lake, and that was only the water-gathering team, under the watchful eyes of a guard.

Drops of rain pelted row after row of the simple wooden benches arranged in a U-shape facing a stage. Behind the stage, the sky darkened over the small patch of sand, framing the dark ten-acre lake, previously used for kayaking and swimming by the summer camp kids before the grid went down, and known for being dangerous—the only shallow bit being on the far side, next to the woods. On this side, it was a straight drop-off with eight-feet-deep water.

A low rumbling of distant thunder filled their ears.

The soggy imprisoned refugees slowly filed in, full of

trepidation, one after the other, filling up the seats, followed by a now-deafening boom of thunder that had moved directly overhead. On one row, more than twenty cabin-mates of the TWO gang all huddled together, separated only by the bikers themselves. Smalls hadn't appeared yet, so Silva guided her girls to the end of the bench, scooting over to leave room for him as she was told to.

Even the rain couldn't cleanse the air, thick with the smell of dirty bodies and a sense of foreboding that curled the toes of every refugee there. Fear wafted from their shabby, wet clothing.

Nothing good ever happened here. This was the place they gathered to hear any crazy new rule, or when either they all, or one person, was in trouble and would be punished. The man in charge treated it as a lesson for them —and entertainment for the militia and the bikers.

In the prior three weeks, they'd seen a handful of punishments meted out: a man's hand smashed with a hammer for stealing food, a woman shaved bald for daring to spit in the face of a guard whose advances she'd refused, a teenage boy stripped naked and paraded out, his hands tied high behind his back for public humiliation. The boy had been accused of slacking; not working hard enough. And finally, the last penalty meted out was a cook who was forced to eat a shit and lettuce sandwich for the alleged crime of watering down the guards' gravy, in order to try to treat his fellow refugees to more—and it was his own shit, made to order right there onto the bed of lettuce, in front of the crowd, to most of their disgust.

They'd also been forced to watch a dozen dog fights...the winner being the one who lived—which was the boss' Pit bull, every single time. The dogs came from outside the camp sometimes, but frequently were brought in by unsuspecting refugees...the same people who now sat on the benches. The violent deaths of what had been many of their own pets were met with gasps and tears from nearly the entire crowd of refugees, and with claps and whistles from the militia and the gang.

The canine bodies were never seen again, and many suddenly hadn't felt like eating their rations for the next few days.

The crowd settled and Cutter strode up to the stage, his face a mask of rage. Lightning cracked as he pulled a bedraggled and muddy Puck with a firm grip on his arm along with him, the boy wincing in pain.

Puck squinted through the onslaught and looked out over the crowd, his eyes searching. "Graysie?" he yelled, while the crowd murmured amongst themselves. "Graysie?"

Cutter cuffed him on the head, and Puck ducked away from the painful slap. "Shut up. She's not here," he ordered. "and she can't hear you—yet."

A guard stepped up, handing Cutter a megaphone and Cutter wasted no time. "Dearly beloved, we are gathered here today...oh wait...that's next week. Okay, so here's the deal. See this kid?" He pointed at a frightened Puck, whose face was streaming with water; a downpour of tears and rain. "We, out of the kindness of our hearts, offered him *safety* and *sanctuary* here at the camp, and do you know how he *repaid* us?"

The crowd was silent, but Puck spoke up. "That's not true. No one was nice to me!"

His retort was met with another wet slap across the head.

Cutter continued. "He shot my nephew."

"No, I didn't!"

Cutter backhanded Puck, knocking him to the ground.

He put his boot on his back, holding him in place. "He shot my nephew, and killed him. Now, what have I told you all over and over would happen if someone raised a hand to a guard?"

The crowd murmured, their voices lost in the storm.

"I can't hear you!" Cutter roared, his veins bulging from his neck.

The guards stood at attention, the rain dripping off the bills of their caps, gripping their rifles in warning as encouragement to the crowd for the right answer.

"Eye for an eye," they quickly roared back in unison, their faces troubled.

Cutter removed his foot, followed by a grunt from Puck, and he paced across the shiny stage in a powerful walk, sending even the puddles scattering in fright. He yelled at the crowd. "That's right. We *can't* have that sort of trouble going unpunished here. If we did, soon this camp would be full of chaos, just like *out there*." He pointed to some faraway place, and as if the heavens themselves heard him, a crack of lightning lit the sky.

The crowd flinched as one.

He stopped pacing. "Now, I'm not a total monster." He paused to check the response from the drenched crowd.

It was crickets. No one dared to deny it.

He chuckled, the sound harsh and humorless, and continued, "No, I'm a generally nice guy. It's been explained to me by my partner, Smalls, that this one here isn't too bright." Cutter tapped his own head. "All the lights on, but nobody home sorta thing going on."

The guards laughed.

Cutter looked out at the crowd. "Smalls? You out there?"

Smalls didn't surface.

"Okay...well, Smalls asked me for a compromise, and we

made a deal. So, here's what I'm gonna do. This kid was followed in by his sister, and get this... his pet *donkey*. A big ole hairy ass! Apparently, he loves them *both* very much... just like I loved my nephew; the *son* of my *dear* little sister, who is no longer with us. My *only sister*, who I made a promise to take care of her *only* child."

He paused for effect, dropping his head and slowly shaking it as he looked at the wooden floor beneath him. Finally, he looked up, and the rain beat down on his angry face. "I hate to break a fucking promise."

The guards all nodded in ridiculous agreement. Not a one there had ever kept a single promise to a single refugee. Every one of them, including Cutter, was well-known to be lying bastards.

"I can't keep my promise to my sister to protect my nephew anymore...but I can keep my promise to *you*!" he pointed out at the crowd. "There *will* be an eye for an eye today."

He waved his arm, and the sound of engines followed.

Puck raised his head, looking for the source of the sound.

Two pieces of equipment—the Bobcat and the tractor—rolled into view onto the sand...both holding their buckets up high. The buckets were equipped with long chains, that led down to large metal cages. One cage was bigger than the other.

Puck scrambled to his feet to face his horror.

In one cage, Jenny bounced back and forth against the iron rails, losing her balance, braying and bellowing in angry fright, her tail twitching in the wind, as the cage swung from the heavy chain.

In the other cage, Graysie was tied to the metal framework from the bottom, with a rope around her waist. Each of her arms were spread wide, tied to the sides at the wrists. Her hands tightly gripped the bars to balance herself as her cage swung to and fro. Her red hair blew around her and her green eyes stared out defiantly until she found Puck.

Their eyes met as the machines positioned the cages directly over the deep end of the lake.

An anguished cry ripped from Puck's throat as he dropped back to his muddy knees. He reached out, stretching his arm toward them, his dirt-covered bloody bandaged hand grabbing at empty air.

Graysie proudly lifted her chin, and shook her head at him, as one lone tear slid down her cheek.

38

CAMP

TUCKER SNAPPED, and exploded from the amphitheater bleachers like a wild Indian, hopping over the last row of refugees and launching himself at the stage, as Katie screamed, "No!"

She was held back by her daughters as the crowd gasped in horror.

He flew into the guard on stage, dropping him with a roundhouse kick, and then plowed into Cutter, taking him down in a fast tackle and roll, ending up on top of the man, pinning down his shoulders with his knees. He grabbed him by both ears and beat his head into the wet, wooden floor. "You. Sick. Fucker. What. The. Fuck. Is. Wrong. With. You?" he screamed, his shaggy hair falling forward, punctuating every word with a jerk of his head, and the boom of Cutter's skull hitting the floor.

The guards dashed to Cutter's side, knocking Tucker off with a barrage of rifle butts. Puck quickly shook off his surprise at seeing Tucker, and hurriedly scooted across the wet wooden floor on his knees, trying but failing, to cover

Tucker with his own body, taking several hard jabs with the painful stocks himself.

But it was useless, there were too many, and the guard that Tucker had kicked recovered quickly and hurried over to deliver a crushing stomp to Tucker's foot.

The snap of bones was loud enough to hear, even over the storm.

Tucker bucked Puck off and jerked into a sitting position, wildly screaming and grabbing his foot. His eyes went wide with crazy.

Puck moved fast, sliding behind and wrapping his arms around Tucker in a bear hug, his long legs spread out alongside Tucker's. "Don't move, Mr. Tucker. They'll hurt you more," he whined. "These are *bad* people," he whispered into his ear.

Puck kept his own head down on Tucker's shoulder, and hid his eyes in fright. He hung on, squeezing Tucker's chest and pulling him tightly against his own.

Tucker frenziedly shook his shoulders, trying to push Puck off, but the boy desperately held on, trying to save Jake's friend.

Nat, one of the bikers, stormed the stage and pushed through the guards, standing over them. "You've went and lost your mind now."

Tucker finally pushed Puck away with a sharp elbow to the ribs, and glared up at the man with eyes full of maddening pain and thoughts of revenge. He smiled through bloody teeth. He recognized him from Curt's house... "Oh you? I know you, *cousin*...you fucking liar. And you have *no* idea how right you are. Ask your cousin how batshit crazy I am! Oh wait...you can't. We kicked leaves over his sorry ass."

Nat gritted his teeth as Tucker laughed manically. "What'd Curt do?"

"Killed a baby," Tucker spit at him. "We caught him hoarding baby formula—and as you know, and more. You were there."

Nat shook his head. "You stupid asshole. That baby milk came from *your* people. Maybe you should've asked your sidekick. Is his wife named *Penny?* He picked it up from *her* garage just before I got there. From what Curt said, she'd been hoarding it, and was too afraid to give it up after all that time. He traded his silence for *some* of the food she had, but he told me he was taking that formula straight to the baby."

Tucker's mouth dropped open, spilling a long line of pink saliva to the floor. "Kenny did this?"

Nat shook his head at the bloody man. "His wife did, so I'm sure he knew..." He held a hand down to his boss, pulling Cutter up off the floor. He pointed at Tucker. "Let me kill this fucker, Boss."

Cutter was enraged... spitting mad. He violently shrugged Nat away and pulled his pistol. He stood over Tucker and Puck with murder in his eyes, the gun pressed firmly against Tucker's forehead, his finger on the trigger.

The crowd gasped and Katie and their daughters screamed in anguish.

"Wait," Tucker said calmly, and grinned, looking all the world like a bloody jack o' lantern. A river of blood dripped down his chin—and another low rumbling of distant thunder filled their ears.

Cutter hesitated...

"Shoot me now, and consider his debt paid." Tucker pointed at Puck. "I'm his people. An eye for an eye—your rule. Let him and the girl go. And the donkey."

Cutter considered it, his eyes narrowed. After a pregnant pause, he slid his gun into the holster. "Get him up and take him to the dog pen," he ordered the guards. "No use wasting a good show. We'll bring him back here tomorrow for his punishment, but today, we're going to finish *this*."

Tucker scrambled with fury to get up, and Puck fought to keep him down.

"Noooo!" Tucker screamed. "Do it now. Pull the trigger…" The guards pulled him away from Puck, his feet dragging behind him, his face full of tormented pain. "Let those kids go," he screamed over his shoulder as they dragged him up the trail toward the camp.

Cutter laughed and pointed at Puck. "Bring the boy over here."

With an army of angry eyes watching, he marched over between the tractor and the Bobcat, both parked where Cutter—or Puck, rather—would have easy access to the joysticks that lowered the buckets. Puck was dragged behind Cutter and dropped at his feet on the sand.

Cutter swiped the water from his face. "Payday. Pay up, bitch. Choose."

Puck tilted his head. "Choose what?"

"To live…or to die." The monster of a man pointed to the lever on each piece of equipment. "You need to push one of these levers. Whichever one you push will lower the cage its holding into the lake. The one you choose, will die." He paused. "But, the good news is…the other lives."

Puck slowly turned and looked at Graysie and Jenny, hanging precariously over the deep, dark water. Jenny returned his gaze with frightened big brown eyes. She tossed her head at Puck, and he felt his heart clinch.

Jenny loved him. She saved him from the fire. She was

his only friend before GrayMan found him. And she loved him best of everybody.

He looked to Graysie.

She sat as still as a statue, the wind now gone. Her clothes were soaked and she shivered, in spite of the heat. Her long hair hung in wet, red tendrils to her face. She shook it away, revealing sorrowful eyes peeking through.

Graysie was his friend, too. And she called him her brother now.

He weighed his choices. Jenny was an *animal*. Graysie was a *human*.

But even GrayMan had said, 'Sometimes animals are better than people. They're our family...' he remembered GrayMan telling that to Tucker, so it must be true.

It was okay to love Jenny more than he did some people.

He loved her *lots* more than he did Mama Dee.

But he loved Graysie, too.

His head filled with a loud buzzing sound.

The sound of angry bees, smothering any clear thought from escaping.

Puck shook his head. "No!" He stomped his foot onto the sand and pointed his finger down, in a full-blown tantrum. "Take them down!"

Cutter waved the guards over. Two men in fatigues took a knee, each aiming scary guns at a different cage. "I'm going to count to ten. If you don't push one of these levers by one, they *both* die with a bullet to the head."

Puck looked at the men in fright and followed the point of their rifles. He sunk down to the sand on his knees, his head in his hands.

Cutter started the countdown. "Ten...nine..."

A lone voice, full of anguish equal to his own, sailed

across the wind. "Puck, push Jenny's lever. Let Graysie live," Katie cried out, through her tears.

"Noooo," he roared back, his eyes darting to Jenny.

He was supposed to *protect* Jenny. He couldn't let her be dropped into the dark water of the lake, weighted down by the bars while she struggled to get out of a cage. She wouldn't know how to open it! He couldn't stand the thought of her head slowly being buried in water, of her lungs filling with it. Drowning...

He couldn't do it.

"Eight...seven...

"Then you choose to kill your sister?" she yelled, trying to explain it to Puck so that he truly understood.

Cutter nodded in delight.

Puck looked at Graysie in confusion and tried to push past the angry noise in his head. She wasn't his sister...but he wanted her to be.

"Six."

This was so confusing. Why wasn't anyone stopping this? Where were the good adults?

His head swiveled around, trying to find Katie in the crowd.

He couldn't see her.

"Five."

"Wait!" Puck yelled. His counting wasn't all that good, especially backward, but he knew time was running out.

"Four."

Puck held his hands out wide in appeal, his knees digging into the sand. "Let *me* inside the cage. Let the girls go," he pleaded.

Cutter ignored him.

"Three"

"Please!" Puck begged. "I can't decide!"

The men readied their rifles, earning a panicked jerk from Puck. He flew to his feet looking left and right at the levers, his eyes wide, then up to Graysie and Jenny...back and forth, back and forth...

"Two."

Puck nearly buckled with another sob as he desperately reached for a lever, the metal wet, his fingers slipping the first time. He took a deep breath, swallowing down his terror and regret.

"I'm sorry," he yelled up to the cages. "So, so, sorry..."

Cutter's lips pursed to shape the word, 'one' and announce a violent end to the countdown, but before he could, Puck pushed the lever with all his might.

A cage dropped into the water with a huge splash.

The crowd gasped as one, and then fell silent.

Puck crumpled back to his knees, his hands crossed over his head, and sobbed.

39

CAMP

GABBY, Tina and Tarra stayed behind, guarding the truck a half mile away, while six figures ran across the soggy ground toward the fence at the far end of the camp. Grayson and Jake took the lead. The guys from the MAG group: Pete, John, Ralph and Chuck brought up the rear.

Jake tripped and nearly fumbled with the bolt-cutters, recovering quickly and quietly cursing his bad leg. He hopped forward a few steps, trying to compensate for his limp.

They reached the fence and spread out in a line along the wire, weapons raised and ready while Jake worked on cutting it, soon opening a gap wide enough for them to slip through. Quietly, they eased through it one at a time, spreading out the same way on the other side in a holding pattern to wait for Jake, who struggled through last, pulling the fence together before they all quietly ran through the rain toward the first guard tower, using the random small cabins and trees for cover.

The group spread out, sloshing through a field, and then melting into the gloom of the storm until soon the only person Grayson could see was Jake, who crouched beside him on the side of a blood-soaked lean-to. He held up a closed fist and then peeked around the corner, grimacing at the sight of a dead orange cat hanging on a crimson-colored hook.

The guard's attention was somewhere else and Grayson murmured his thanks to the sky, and then ran for the tower, keeping low and praying the guard wouldn't turn around before he reached it.

His prayer went unanswered.

Pop pop pop pop pop

A heavy machine gun opened up, sending dirt and mud flying all around Grayson. He tucked his head and ran at full speed, throwing himself into a slide to reach the underside of the tower on his stomach as if he was stealing third base, just as Ralph returned fire, with a barrage of full metal jacket, shredding the man's shirt. The guard fell over the side, thumping to the ground next to Grayson, his eyes wide open in death.

Grayson waved the group forward again, clutching an unfamiliar M4 to his chest—the MAG group had loaned it to him so he could leave enough of their big guns with the women guarding the truck—and they jogged, making their way through a deserted campground, Jake a few steps behind him.

Where is everybody?

There wasn't a soul to be seen on this side of camp so they pushed forward, Grayson's heart in his throat, as he tried to push down his panic. If he lost Graysie or Puck, he didn't know what he'd do. What if the rogue militia had moved them to a new location?

There were no signs of life, until they reached a dog pen.

Grayson nudged Jake. "Those are Tucker's dogs," he whispered.

The dogs ran to the gate and Jake nodded, reaching through the fence and giving the scared pups a quick rub. A Pit Bull huddled in the back, curious but scared. On the other side of the pen, they were surprised to see a man laying crumpled and broken, face-down on the cement.

Slowly, his head raised.

It was Tucker.

"Tucker!" Jake gasped. "Are you okay?"

Tucker smiled a bloody, broken smile, and pointed at his foot, which by that time was swollen and purple. His sock and shoe lay discarded next to him.

Grayson shook his head. "Shit. Looks like he's hanging in there like a hair in a biscuit."

Tucker pointed. "Go...they have Puck and Graysie down at the lake. *Hurry!* They're in trouble."

Jake was conflicted. "Grayson...the bolt cutters. I left them at the fence back there. I can run back and get them and we can get Tucker out of here."

"No!" Grayson ordered fiercely. "He's safe in there. Let's get the kids out first."

Tucker agreed with him, and Jake promised his friend he'd be back, and moved to catch up with the group. Soon, they came upon another tower, with another distracted guard, watching something happening through the trees. Before Grayson could decide what to do, Pete fired a burst and the man went down hard, his lights going out before he hit the ground, his head a gruesome mess.

Pete glanced at Grayson and shrugged. "I called dibs on that one."

They scattered again, this time the MAG group splitting

off from Grayson and Jake, who continued forward toward the tree line, the direction that Tucker had pointed them, and the same direction that had held both the guard's attention, when they abruptly came upon a trio of men in fatigues a hundred feet away that had been quietly standing at the edge of the woods, smoking cigarettes and peering down the trail. One of the guards turned, spotting the two men.

The guard sounded the alarm, bringing his rifle up.

Grayson and Jake both dived separate ways. Grayson hit the ground and rolled behind a low metal cart onto his back, cringing at the long rattle that split the air around him. He flipped over onto his stomach and lifted his M4, feeling for the fire selector switch, and putting it in three-round burst mode. His finger tightened on the trigger and the gun barked, slamming into his first target, and nearly demolishing it.

A fucking tree.

The guard ran at him.

He took a deep breath, exhaled, and let it out, pulling the trigger again, taking his time in spite of the man clearing the gap between them, still squeezing his own trigger. This time, the man spun around as though he'd forgotten something, and then crumpled to the ground.

Grayson's lead had struck just below the man's nose, taking out the back of his skull, blowing bits of blood, bone and hair behind him.

His partners dived behind a small building, still returning fire at Grayson, but they were soon followed by the lob of a grenade from Chuck's pack.

Jake ran to Grayson, pulling him up off the ground. "Let's go! Run!"

Grayson jogged forward a few steps, fighting off the shock of just killing a man—*another* man. His mind wandered, flashing images of the others he'd killed since the collapse, most recently Curt. What was he turning into? —*boom*—the grenade detonated, surprising Grayson and Jake with its force and sending them to the ground, staring in shock at the sudden blaze of red and orange lighting up the sky, despite the rain.

The boom of the blast stole the show from the angry roll of thunder.

One man stumbled out, black and blood-red trails streaming down his face, carried swiftly by the rain. A bloody nub waved from his right shoulder. He swayed and meandered left to right, drunkenly hurrying down the trail with his lifeblood streaming out behind him.

John emerged from nowhere, stepping behind the man, pushing his rifle over his shoulder to hang from a sling and instead pulling one of his pistols from the low-slung holsters he liked to wear, like an old west gunfighter.

Quickly, he put an end to the injured man and silently waved Grayson and Jake forward. He stepped off into the woods, disappearing in the dense brush, with the rest of his crew.

Jake and Grayson ran down the trail toward the lake, and toward the firefight that had started without them. All hell broke loose as a spray of bullets began to fly, sending the refuges running in a panic up the trail, right into them.

The crowd parted around them, a pulsing human wave of panic flowing uphill, and Jake saw Katie and the girls. She broke away from the crowd and ran into his arms, nearly falling to her knees. "Jake! They took Tucker. They broke his foot," she sobbed.

Jake helped her stand. "I saw him. He's in a dog kennel, that way..." he pointed. "Take the girls. We'll come back there for you. Now go!"

"But my boys—"

"—we'll find them too, just go, Katie!" Jake yelled at her. "Listen to me!"

Kenny and Penny ran up, with eyes full of panic and terror. "Jake! Can you take us with you?" Kenny panted, his arm wrapped tight around his wife's shoulders.

Katie shoved past Jake, and shoved Penny. "You! How could you? We trusted you!"

Jake looked at the two women in confusion. Penny hung her head, and Kenny tightened his grip on her. Coming up the trail he saw Xander and his family. There'd be no room for all these people in the truck.

Katie spit on the ground in front of Kenny and Penny. "Leave them, Jake. You don't want lying, hoarding *murderers* near *your* people," Katie snarled, to Jake's shock.

Bullets ricocheted off the trees and everyone ducked.

Jake was losing sight of Grayson. "I've got to go! Y'all *run*! You're gonna get shot...we'll figure this out later." Jake pushed through them and hurried after Grayson, who hadn't broken his stride in his quest to find his daughter and Puck, even amidst a tsunami of slugs peppering the forest floor and the trees around them.

40

CAMP

Grayson stood at the edge of the madness for just a moment, looking for Graysie, when splinters flew past his head like arrows. He ducked and watched as Chuck, from the MAG group, ushered the refugees off of the bleachers, hurrying them away from the fight. He swallowed down bile at the number of angry, red number 2's he saw on the women's arms.

A gunshot rang out from Pete, and Grayson ducked, and then cringed as he watched an ink-covered man get his head vaporized.

Ralph was on the other side of the amphitheater, hurrying toward an unsuspecting guard who was squatting on the ground, busy trying to belatedly load a magazine for the empty gun he now held, his back against the low stage wall. Ralph crept up on him, bending over the man with a Ka-bar knife and adding a red smiley-face to his neck.

John jumped up to the stage, high-fiving Ralph and exchanging the red paint with a splash. They both stood tall on the stage, backlit by a display of lightning, looking for more enemy to dispatch.

There wasn't a one to see...the rest had tucked tail and ran.

And then Grayson saw Graysie.

He growled and his vision clouded.

His *little girl*...hanging up in the air, wet and fragile under an onslaught of rain in a metal cage over a dark and brewing lake. Puck was clinging to the chain like a monkey, trying to shimmy down to her with one good hand while his injured hand dripped a solid beat of blood, now free of its bandage.

A second shot of adrenaline hit his heart and he willed himself to breathe and then ran full speed toward the beach, with Jake limping behind, his leg almost giving out by now.

They reached the beach and Jake jumped into the Bobcat, yelling at Puck to hang on tight. He slammed down the safety cage, hit the hydraulic engagement button and maneuvered the controls to spin the machine, swinging the bucket to hang over the sand where he slowly lowered it, leaving the heavy chain taut—with Puck still wrapped around it—so that it didn't fall onto Graysie and hurt her.

Grayson ran to the cage, and slammed the door open.

He gasped.

Graysie's hands were tied. Her body was tied. She would've drowned had someone lowered her into the water. As Puck dropped heavily into the sand beside him, jumping from the chain, Grayson quickly pulled out his knife and ripped through the ropes, freeing Graysie and pulling her from the cage, and to his chest.

He kissed the top of her head, squeezing her tightly to his heart and then pulled away from her, looking her over from head to toe. "Are you okay, Graysie? Did they hurt you?"

Puck grabbed Grayson's arm. "Jenny!" he yelled, pointing at the water.

Grayson spared a glance, seeing nothing but a chain coming out of the water hooked to the bucket of a tractor. He ignored Puck, seizing Graysie's sleeve and pushing it up, looking for the mark of these beasts. He exhaled in relief to see nothing but a smatter of the precious freckles she was born with on her milky-white skin.

"GrayMan!" Puck yelled over the thunder. "We have to help Jenny!"

Finally, he had his attention, but before he could make heads or tails of what the boy was saying, the man they'd met once before showed up, a chilling smile on his scarred face, he stood on the edge of the beach aiming a gun at them.

Without warning, the man screamed, "An eye for an eye," and opened fire, sending a fountain of sand up around their ankles.

They dived behind the machinery as bullets sang against the metal.

A long rattle answered the song, coming from Gabby's friends as they unloaded on the man...putting Jake and Grayson and the kids into a crossfire that stopped almost as soon as it started. Like a ghost, Cutter had disappeared into the trees, evading death again.

The sky opened up once again in fury, dropping torrential rain.

John ran through the sand, waving to Grayson and his group. "Let's go. We've got to get out of here before he comes back with more men."

The group of eight ran the opposite way from where the man had faded into the trees, and forged a trail of their own. Grayson held Graysie's hand, pulling her along with him, as

Jake pushed and pulled a fighting Puck...who was insistent they not leave Jenny behind.

There was no time for Jenny...or time to listen to his words even. Their lives were on the line and they ran, breaking out of the woods near the fence line where they'd come in. The men from the mag group hurried through the gap in the wire that Jake had cut, holding it open for Grayson and his family.

Grayson nudged Graysie through first, then Puck, and then waited for Jake, who stood looking the opposite way, the bolt cutters back in his hand. "Come on, Jake...get your ass through here. We gotta go!"

Jake yelled back, "I can't leave Tucker and Katie and the kids!"

"The hell you can't! There's no way you have time to go cut him out and get them all back here. The guards will be on us like fly on shit in a matter of minutes. We have to get to the truck!"

Jake shook his head. "Go without me then. I'm not leaving him again. I promised him and Katie I'd come back."

"For fucks sake, Jake! I can't leave you behind. Come the fuck on," he yelled angrily, impatiently holding the gap open, his boots sinking into the ground that was now a soggy puddle of mud.

Jake swallowed hard. "It's best I stay here with them anyway, Grayson. I have to get clean."

Grayson swiped away the water streaming down his face. "What the hell are you talking about?" he yelled over the storm.

"Your painkillers. I took them. I'm an addict."

Grayson stared at him in astonishment. It was a fine time to drop this shit on him. He'd wondered where his pills had gone, and he'd noticed Jake acting weird—actually since before the grid went down. This explained so much... Him disappearing for hours at a time. Sweating before the sun was even up high, the shakes, the headaches, the nausea.

He'd been blind to it all, but now he saw...and fuck if it wasn't bad timing to see.

"Doesn't matter, Jake. We'll deal with that at home."

Jake shook his head. "No. I've tried. I don't trust myself. I'm putting everyone in jeopardy. I'll dry out here, locked up where I can't get any, and I can look out for Tucker and his family while I'm doing it."

Grayson stood up to his full height, letting go of the fence. Puck and Graysie stood on the other side, shivering in fear. "Stop it, Jake. Get your ass through this fence right now..." he said, taking long strides toward his brother-in-law.

Jake put up his hand. "I mean it, Grayson. I'm not going without them. Leave us."

Grayson kicked the ground, sending up a splash of mud and water. "Holy fucking shit balls son of a pecker-headed bastard!!" he cursed.

He grabbed Jake in a bear hug, squeezed him tight, and then let him go. He turned, with a tear in his eye and scurried through the fence without another glance behind him.

41

CAMP

Grayson listened with relief to the truck rumble off, carrying the women and Puck safely home, and then turned and ran like his ass was on fire, with the guys of the mag group right behind him, back toward the fence.

He breathed heavily as he struggled through his fatigue to put one foot in front of the other. That was their only ride, and now it was gone. The MAG group had chosen to leave their own truck at the farm to save fuel. It was only a ten-mile hike home though...and he hoped to be able to find the strength to make it there by nightfall. But his choice was made.

Family first.

He admired the mag group, who'd made a promise to Gabby long before the grid went down to always have her back—or her family's. It helped that these men seemed to enjoy this sort of thing, too, and refused to leave Jake behind as well.

Grayson tucked his face down and watched the ground to protect him from the needle-like assault of rain pelting against his flesh, and a misstep that might leave him stranded out here with a broken ankle and no ride home.

He turned the corner and slid to a stop in the wet dirt. The guys slid in beside him.

Tied to the fence was a wet, dirty and scruffy donkey. The ass' legs were caked in thick mud all the way up to her stomach.

Jenny snorted a happy hello and stepped out as far as the rope she was tied to allowed, her hooves making a sucking sound as she pulled them out of the mud one at a time.

Behind her, Smalls carried Jake over his shoulder, just reaching the fence before he was discovered by Grayson, and the guys.

Grayson raised his M4 in unison with John, Pete, Chuck and Ralph's guns. "Put him down, Smalls," he ordered.

"I intend to. He's heavy as shit," Smalls loudly answered.

The mammoth of a man laid Jake in front of the hole as though he were nothing but a rag doll, and then leaned into the fence, pushing the gap open, and tried to feed Jake through it to Grayson... and failing at moving the limp man. "Help me," he grunted.

While the guys kept their guns on Smalls, Grayson dropped his own, and bent over at the fence, reaching through and grabbing Jake under the shoulders. He pulled with all his might.

Jake's pant leg was caught on the jagged wire, but his body remained lifeless.

"Like trying to shove a wet noodle up a wildcat's ass," Grayson mumbled.

"Pull," Smalls said, as he pushed.

Grayson gave a big tug and Jake's pants ripped, setting him free, but leaving a bloody gash on his shin. They flew backward, Jake landing on his lap, he on his back. He quickly pushed him off and sat up, reaching for his gun.

The men of the mag group stepped forward in warning.

Smalls shook his head. "No need for that. I knocked him out just to bring him here. Figured he'd come to his senses when he woke up, and go on home. It's the best I could do. Tucker isn't leaving. He told Jake as much. His boys are outside the camp right now and he won't go without them. I'll watch over him and his family—and the rest of your friends."

"Why are you doing this for us?"

Smalls dropped his head for a moment, and then looked up.

"I talked Cutter outta putting a bullet in that boy's brain, and connived him into the lake deal with a half-assed plan to jump in and open one of those cages. Ended up fighting that fat ass there." He pointed at a forgiving Jenny who finally brayed her thanks to him. "But I did it for *Edith*. Tell Elmer I'm truly sorry I couldn't stop what happened. I tried. I would've taken that bullet for that old lady. She didn't deserve what happened to her." He swallowed hard.

He nodded toward Jake. "And I owed him one. He set me loose, back at your farm."

Grayson's fingers found his rifle, and he gripped the gun, his brother-in-law still out cold. He narrowed his eyes at Smalls. "Now what?"

Smalls stood up from his crouch, the fence between them.

"Now you haul ass home—and fast."

"The rest of them coming after us?" Grayson questioned, looking beyond Smalls out into the camp for the militia.

"No, but something else is. You need to find cover quick. I'm not sure you'll make it all the way back to your farm, unless you got a ride out there? This grid going down was just the first phase of a coordinated attack. I've got good intelligence that says nuclear blackmail is next. There's a bomb coming, with threats to set off more unless demands were met."

He paused.

"And demands haven't been met."

Grayson swallowed hard. "When is this supposed to happen?"

Smalls looked up into the stormy sky. "Half past *now*. Y'all better run like the wind."

The End

My Shit (hit the fan) List

To get on my Shit List, where you'll hear about each new release of The SHTF Series, and get inside information on my other post-apoc books, take thirty seconds to sign up here for my monthly newsletter. I don't need your name, you'll never be spammed or shared, and you can easily unsubscribe at any time with one click. To read book 4: Wait Like a Stone, click here.

WAIT LIKE A STONE
BOOK FOUR
SHTF
AUTHOR OF THE LET ME GO SERIES
L.L. AKERS

SAUTEED DANDELION GREENS RECIPE

1 lb clean dandelion greens, torn into 4-inch pieces
1 teaspoon salt
2 tablespoons olive oil
1 tablespoon butter
1/2 onion, thinly sliced
1/4 teaspoon red pepper flakes
2 cloves garlic, minced
salt and ground black pepper to taste
1 tablespoon grated Parmesan cheese (optional)

1. Soak dandelion greens in a large bowl of cold water with 1 teaspoon salt for 10 minutes. Drain.
2. Bring a large pot of water to a boil with 1 teaspoon salt. Cook greens until tender, 3 to 4 minutes. Drain and rinse with cold water until chilled.
3. Heat olive oil and butter in a large skillet over medium heat; cook and stir onion and red pepper flakes until onion is tender, about 5 minutes. Stir in garlic until garlic is fragrant, about 30 seconds more. Increase heat to medium-high and add dandelion greens. Continue to cook and stir until liquid is evaporated, 3 to 4 minutes. Season with salt and black pepper.
4. Sprinkle greens with Parmesan cheese and serve warm or hot

BOOKS BY L.L. AKERS

The SHTF Series

Book 1: *Fight Like a Man*

Book 2: *Shoot Like a Girl*

Book 3: *Run Like the Wind*

Book 4: Wait Like a Stone

Other Books:

A Heart for War, a novella

O'Donnell Classic Western Collection:

Broken Bow

Dismal River

Blood on the Republican

Man on Pine Ridge

The ***Let Me Go Series***, written as Lisa Akers,

The origin stories of the SHTF Characters:

The Girl in the Box

The Girl on the Swing

The Girl in the Sea

The Girl in Red

HANG OUT WITH OTHER READERS/PREPPERS

Want free loot and a fun hangout?

Join our Facebook group: DD12 – The Dirty Dozen Post Apoc Army. We're twelve good friends who all write post apocalypse, prepper, and/or survival fiction. The group is about the books, prepping, survival and lots of good fun—sense of humor strongly advised.

...and we give away *free prepping/survival loot to our readers*—and lots of it.

DD12 - Dirty Dozen Post Apoc Army

And finally, *please*... by all that is holy, go to your favorite retailer and leave a fair review. Indie authors rely on word of mouth and reviews to get noticed by other readers.

Made in the USA
Columbia, SC
30 July 2023